MW01133222

from Nancy March 2023

KINGDOM GARDENS

S. Renee Felder

WESTBOW
PRESS®
A DIVISION OF THOMAS NELSON
& ZONDERVAN

WestBow Press books may be ordered through booksellers or by contacting:

WestBow Press
A Division of Thomas Nelson & Zondervan
1663 Liberty Drive
Bloomington, IN 47403
www.westbowpress.com
844-714-3454

Because of the dynamic nature of the Internet, any web addresses or
links contained in this book may have changed since publication and
may no longer be valid. The views expressed in this work are solely those
of the author and do not necessarily reflect the views of the publisher,
and the publisher hereby disclaims any responsibility for them.

Any people depicted in stock imagery provided by Getty Images are
models, and such images are being used for illustrative purposes only.
Certain stock imagery © Getty Images.

Unless otherwise indicated, scripture quotations are taken from
the Amplified® Bible, Copyright © 1954, 1958, 1962, 1964, 1965,
1987 by The Lockman Foundation. Used by permission.

Scripture quotations marked NKJV are taken from the New King James Version.
Copyright © 1982 by Thomas Nelson, Inc. Used by permission. All rights reserved.

ISBN: 978-1-6642-8410-4 (sc)
ISBN: 978-1-6642-8411-1 (e)

Library of Congress Control Number: 2022921204

Print information available on the last page.

WestBow Press rev. date: 01/06/2023

CONTENTS

EDITORS

Zoe Burkett

Denise Felder

Dr. Carmen Smith

ACKNOWLEDGEMENTS

I want to thank my local prayer team, led by Tammy Lawrence, the Victory Fellowship congregation, the Victory Fellowship prayer team led by Brian Chirhart, and my family for their continued support and prayers on this journey.

I thank Zoe Burkett for her creative insights and suggestions during the editing process of the journey.

I thank Denise Felder, my insightful sister, who asked some of the critical questions that were taken into consideration and enhanced the story's voice.

I thank Dr. Carmen Smith, for her encouragement, wisdom, and gentle probing of sensitive topics in the editing process.

Lastly, I thank Karin Jones, my weekly prayer partner, for her prophetic insights and personal prayers, which have helped to keep me centered.

PROLOGUE

When I completed *The Bridge, Moving from Increasing Chaos to Future Peace*, I thought at the time that it would be the one and only book I would write and publish. This thought was contrary to the number of prophetic words I had been given about writing multiple books. The creative and disciplined process of writing was new to me and, to be honest, a difficult journey. But I accomplished what the Lord asked me to do, so I thought I was finished with that part of my journey.

I wrote and published the first book just before COVID-19 hit the world, and we all went into hibernation, in a manner of speaking. So, the trajectory of what was supposed to happen with the book was delayed.

When things started returning to normal, I started looking for a local congregation to be a part of. Following the leading of the Lord, I ended up at a church where the prophetic word was commonplace. The Pastor, Lonnie Parton, called my name and asked me if I was a writer. I said I had written a book, and he prophesied, among other things, that I had multiple books to write. As I mentioned, he was not the first to tell me this. But, being human and remembering how hard it was with the first book, I put the prophetic word on a proverbial shelf.

Several months later, I attempted to move forward in some other areas I felt the Lord was telling me to do. Still, I felt stuck and unable to move forward, and I could not figure out why.

One Sunday, Pastor Lonnie asked people to raise their hands if they felt like they had a purpose but were feeling stuck or held back. I raised my hand. Pastor Lonnie looked at me and told me that I was supposed to write and told me to start writing.

This time, I took what he said to heart and started praying after repenting from not wanting to do what I was told. Once I repented and yielded to the Lord, the Lord wanted me to write about how to prepare for the economic, financial, and governmental changes that were coming to America.

In my mind, I assumed I would write about the financial future since the first book was about the collapse of the banking system. It was a logical first step since it was something I was more familiar with in the natural. So, I felt more comfortable writing about what the Lord has shown me in this area. But the Lord did not say financial. I heard, "Write about preparing for the food shortage." Food? I don't know much about food except how to eat. Why food? I asked Him. He said, *"Because it will be the biggest adjustment the Body of Christ will have to make, and we need to start now."*

But I still felt stuck. I was still trying to figure out the format the book was supposed to take. Then one Sunday, a few weeks later, another church leader, Jim Nichols, preached when Pastor Lonnie was out of town. He taught about the Jewish tallit, the prayer shawl, and how the tallit was used as a personal tabernacle. Jim then instructed some men to come and hold up the tallits above the head of the congregation and invited everyone, including the children, to go underneath. There was such a strong presence of the Holy Spirit underneath the tallit I was under. I felt wrapped in God's glory. God's presence stayed with me for several hours after the service. He was downloading the book into me. Later that afternoon, I knew what form the book was supposed to take. I knew it would be a story, and I knew it would be set 5 years into the future.

Kingdom Gardens is a picture of what our country will look like in the year 2027 based on our country's current trajectory. It is written from the perspective of a young man sent on a journey in search of answers that will help his local community's food insecurity issues. He gave me a blueprint of how the Kingdom on earth can and should operate even amid the coming turmoil in our economy and government. The story gives a glimpse of the continued impact of our current laws and regulations, where they are headed, and the increased tension between some states and the Federal government. The specific states are not mentioned because the fate of each state from God's perspective, has not been decided.

Once I understood the format and received the story plot based on what the Holy Spirit told me, I started researching to see what other prophetic voices were saying about a food shortage. I found prophetic voices familiar to many and some not so familiar speaking on the subject. Among those mentioning food shortages or famine in the United States were Chris Reed, Perry Stone, Joshua Giles, Nita Johnson, Chuck Pierce, and many more. In fact, I was surprised at the number of prophetic voices saying we would suffer from a food shortage in our country. What this tells me is that (1) God is confirming His word through multiple prophetic voices, (2) He wants us to pay attention (3) He wants His people to do something about it.

I believe we can find a part of our strategy for what God's Kingdom people are supposed to do in the story of Joseph found in Genesis chapter 41, summarized below:

Jacob's son, Joseph, was a prophet gifted by God to interpret dreams. God anointed him with wisdom and understanding to make strategic decisions at a critical time in world history. The story of Joseph begins in Genesis 37. In summary, Egypt's Pharaoh received two dreams on the same night that greatly troubled him. Pharaoh inquired of his magicians and wise men. But they could not interpret his dreams. So, they sent for Joseph, who provided the interpretations to Pharaoh.

"And, behold, he stood by the river. Suddenly there came up out of the river seven cows, fine looking and fat; and they fed in the meadow. Then behold, seven other cows came up after them out of the river, ugly and gaunt, and stood by the other cows on the bank of the river. And the ugly and gaunt cows ate up the seven fine-looking and fat cows. So Pharaoh awoke. He slept and dreamed a second time; and suddenly seven heads of grain came up on one stalk, plump and good. Then behold, seven thin heads, blighted by the east wind, sprang up after them. And the seven thin heads devoured the seven plump and full heads. So Pharaoh awoke, and indeed, it was a dream."
Genesis 41:1-7 (NKJV)

Joseph informed Pharaoh that both dreams held the same meaning. He also said that since the dream came twice, the events that were about to take place had been established by God. In other words, it was sure to happen. Egypt and all the land would have seven years of great prosperity followed by seven years of severe famine, and all previous prosperity would be forgotten.

But God didn't just give Joseph the interpretation of Pharaoh's dreams. He also provided the answer to the problem those dreams presented:

"'Now therefore, let Pharaoh select a discerning and wise man, and set him over the land of Egypt. Let Pharaoh do this, and let him appoint officers over the land, to collect one-fifth of the produce of the land of Egypt in the seven plentiful years. And let them gather all the food of those good years that are coming, and store up grain under the authority of Pharaoh, and let them keep food in the cities. Then that food shall be as a reserve for the land for the seven years of famine

which shall be in the land of Egypt; that the land may not perish during the famine.' So the advice was good in the eyes of Pharaoh and in the eyes of all his servants. And Pharaoh said to his servants, 'Can we find such a one as this, a man in whom is the Spirit of God?' Then Pharaoh said to Joseph, 'Inasmuch as God has shown you all this, there is no one as discerning and wise as you.'" **Genesis 41:33-39 (NKJV)**

God gave Joseph a strategy for Egypt – store up enough food and provisions during the coming years of plenty to feed people during the impending famine. Through this strategy, God used Joseph to help all of Egypt and peoples from surrounding nations survive during seven long years of relentless famine.

I do not know how long our food issues will last, but I know the crisis will be prolonged and likely to last several years. In our current times, The Body of Christ is supposed to help our nation survive and thrive through the coming shakings. This will take an intentional, coordinated effort from *ALL* of us.

The Food shortage is one of many areas where God's people are supposed to be a resource. Other areas include housing, finances, nutrition, and medical. Some of these examples are touched on in this book.

Lastly, I hope the story within these pages will spark your interest and help you to determine your part of the Kingdom solution the Lord wants to manifest on the earth.

THE ARRIVAL

*T*HE YEAR IS 2027. IT is a late summer afternoon in the Midwest. The air is humid, with a breeze from the West doing little to cool the temperature under the summer sun's heat. I had just disembarked from the train and headed toward the terminal to meet Mr. Smith, the Kingdom Coordinator for the area. The train ride is long...many stops along the way. But these days, it is one of the few economical ways to travel, with the automobile fuel price fluctuating between $15 and $20 a gallon.

I was excited and nervous at the same time. I was chosen for this assignment because of my parents' background and the training I received from them. My resume indicates that I have experience as a restaurant worker. Front-end as a host and server and in the kitchen as an assistant cook. My travel documents indicate that I am here to interview for a position in one of the chain restaurants in the area. It's the cover story for the real reason why I am here. The state I am visiting does not require travel documents. But my state, where I live, does require them. I will need them for when I return home.

Back at home, my parents used to own a farm. We had a garden just for us, which my mother cultivated. We had all sorts of fruits and vegetables in the summer and fall, including a small apple orchid. We had cattle, chickens, and even a goat. My parents also grew wheat, barley, corn, and soybeans. Everything is so different now. The changes happened so fast… it is like waking up from a bad dream and then realizing it is not a dream.

Walking towards the front of the terminal, I passed at least two checkpoints where people had to check in before boarding the train. I did this also. The redundant checks slowed the boarding process causing the check-in to take about 3 hours. I remember my parents telling me before the 9/11 event when American planes were attacked by terrorists, that people arrived at the airport less than an hour before their flight and still had time to board their plane before it departed. 9/11 changed all of that. The check-in process at the airport became long and tedious. Boarding the trains seems worse since more and more people travel by train rather than fly or drive. The terminal was very congested, and I had to weave through the crowds to baggage claim. I brought one small carry-on, electing not to check any luggage. I heard too many stories of people checking luggage and then having items missing once they arrived at their destination.

I will be here for three nights.

I was told to ask a lot of questions and take copious notes. I made my way to the baggage claim exit. I see a middle-aged man of average height holding a sign with the name 'T. Williams'. I eagerly walk towards him. "Mr. Smith?" I asked.

He looks at me with deliberate eyes and returns the question, "T. Williams?"

"Yes, it's Tom," I said. "It's nice to meet you."

"You as well, Tom. Would you mind showing me your identification and your introduction letter?"

"Yes, of course," I said.

In the moment, I had forgotten that my Kingdom Coordinator, or 'KC' as we affectionately call him, had written an introductory letter. He explicitly told me to present it to Mr. Smith upon my arrival. I pulled out my cell phone from my pocket and opened the app.

The introduction letter is not an actual written document.

It's a cell phone application created with blockchain technology adapted from cryptocurrency. I opened the application and put in the encrypted code I had memorized. Mr. Smith then touched his phone to my phone, and the document was transferred. Mr. Smith put in his encrypted code. Once he did this, a digitalized document showed. He reviewed his copy, looked at me, and gave me a welcoming smile.

"The car is this way," he said.

He turned and began walking across the street to the parking lot. The majority of the cars were either electronic or hybrid. There were a lot of electric bicycles as well, and I even spotted a couple of horses at the far end of the lot. Mr. Smith led me to a blue late-model Tesla. We got in and started driving.

On the drive, Mr. Smith asked me general questions about my background and how I landed this task from KC, our Kingdom Coordinator.

"I was referred by my home group leader. Our group has a successful network of gardens among us. Because of my farming and gardening background, I could train the others in the group. KC wants to expand the network citywide. Food insecurity is increasing in our city."

I turned my head away as my words lingered in the air. "Anyway," I continued. "KC was aware of the success you have here. I understand you knew each other from the past?" I asked.

"Yes." Mr. Smith answered. "He and I went to seminary together; It seems like a lifetime ago. We kept in touch and saw each other over the years at one Christian conference or another. He and I disagreed on future events. He was a patriot at heart and believed in the sovereignty of the United States. Nothing wrong with that, I suppose." He shrugged his shoulders once and continued.

"The problem comes in when you think because our country is so great, nothing will touch us. The United States will continue to stay on top, and no permanent harm will come to us. Nothing to do except pray and pledge our allegiance to our country." Mr. Smith paused and took a deep breath.

"Many people did not expect this food situation to continue to get worse. Every year I would hear someone say, next year will get better. Only it's not just food that is increasingly insecure these days. The 2028 election, I believe, will set in motion some very drastic changes in our country. Many people, including your KC, thought I was too 'doom and gloom' and lacked faith...." Mr. Smith's voice trailed off.

"But faith put me on this course to take action. Anyway, Your KC and I – Larry is his name, reconciled and began a closer friendship about a year ago. You coming here is one of the fruits of our renewed friendship."

We both grew quiet, and I turned to look out the window. There were many boarded-up buildings along the way, and a closer look revealed that most of the closed locations were restaurants. We passed several fast-food chains that were now closed, and we also passed two chain grocery stores that were also boarded up.

Mr. Smith noticed where I was looking. "We only have one chain grocery store left, and they have three locations in the city." Only two chain restaurants left also." He shook his head.

"Even though I knew it was coming, it's still hard to believe it happened. That it *is actually happening*. We have a co-op which includes a restaurant," Mr. Smith continued.

"But it's only open Friday, Saturday, and Sunday. And since today is Friday...this is where we are going."

I smiled in anticipation. Not only to get a chance to experience the restaurant I had heard so much about but also because I was hungry. I had two egg salad sandwiches, 2 peanut butter sandwiches, a single serving of apple sauce, one serving of fruit cocktail, and a thermos of water for the 18-hour journey. All eaten hours ago. The train provided food service, but the prices were out of reach for most people. The lowest price for something to eat on the menu was $40 for cheese fries. A package of sliced cheese in the grocery store was

4

around $30. Of course, the train had premium pricing generally found when traveling. A 16-ounce bottle of water was $25. At home, in the one grocery chain left, a 16-ounce water bottle runs about $15. It's not that water is scarce… it's in a plastic bottle. Due to environmental concerns, my state heavily taxed anything made of plastic or other materials deemed harmful to the environment. So, I brought my own thermos. However, I could only fill it one time after I passed the last check-in at the train station. There were no water fountains on the train.

Although the train ride was 18 hours long, the drive would have only been about 12 hours if I had driven. The many stops and connections along the way extended the journey. Since the demand for train travel has increased, many cargo train cars were converted to accommodate passengers. Routes that previously were used to transport only cargo are now transporting people. I had to transfer a couple of times using these restored routes. The trains on the fixed routes have much fewer amenities.

The network of train travel in some areas of the country had reverted back to how it was in the late 19th and early 20th centuries. The tracks were already laid, so it was just a matter of converting the train cars. I remember hearing about the conversion plans a few years ago. The train conversions were funded by the Infrastructure Bill passed in 2021. Although at the time, the public was unaware that some of the funding would be for cargo train conversions.

DAY 1

The co-op Restaurant

*A*S WE DROVE INTO THE parking lot, I noticed very few cars. There were a couple of golf carts but primarily electric bicycles. Towards the back were several hitching posts for horses and containers for water in front of each post. Also, further away was a shovel and a large closed container to the left side of the posts. It looked like what we had on the farm to shovel manure. Behind the hitching post was a large vegetable garden. Towards the back was a hen house with a walking area for the hens. There looked to be about 30 or so hens. Now I was famished. We parked closer to the restaurant doors and walked inside.

What I saw took my breath away. We were standing in the waiting area, but we could see into the restaurant where we stood. There were multiple tables and chairs, as one would expect in a restaurant. What took my breath away was the décor and how everything was arranged. There were some table and chair sets like you would see in a restaurant, but there were also table and chair sets that traditionally belonged in homes. These dining sets were intermingled throughout the dining area. Some of the tables did not have matching chairs, but it all seemed to work aesthetically. There was another dining area further off to the right, but I could only see a bar with a separate eating area and bar stools.

An electronic menu was on the wall on either side of us and in the dining area. There were 5 meal choices available; chicken vegetable soup, vegan vegetable soup, beef and bean chili, baked chicken with mashed potatoes or roasted fries, and a cheeseburger on sourdough, white or sprouted grain bread. The soups were cup or bowl sizes, and the cheeseburger was four or eight ounces.

"The menu items change weekly and sometimes daily depending on what is available." Mr. Smith explained as we were both gazing at the menu. There were also three choices for dessert, strawberry rhubarb pie, blueberry pie, or baked apples.

We were taken to our seats. The server, Janet, came over to take our orders. I ordered the cheeseburger on toasted sourdough and roasted potatoes. Mr. Smith ordered baked chicken with mashed potatoes. Also included was a salad and our choice of dessert. For our drinks, we both chose water. The restaurant did not offer any sodas. Only coffee, hot tea, iced tea, and water.

"Sometimes there is lemonade, orange juice, apple juice, or a flavored iced tea with various herbs." Mr. Smith was saying. "Every year, we cultivate more summer fruits. We hope to have enough to consume and trade with other Kingdom communities in two years."

Janet brought our water and salads.

"Wow!" I said, my eyes widening at the sight of the salad in front of me. "This salad is so big! And so colorful!"

There were several types of lettuce in the salad ranging in color from a deep purple to a red/green mix. I also spotted spinach, dandelion leaf, cherry tomatoes, shredded carrots, a spattering of red onion, and green and red bell pepper. Janet also brought a tray of serving dishes containing sunflower seeds, dried cranberries, raisins, walnuts, and croutons. On the tray were also several varieties of salad dressing. I chose the vinegar and oil with oregano. I poured it generously onto my salad after adding cranberries, walnuts, and croutons.

I was about to dig in when Mr. Smith raised his hand and said, "Wait. In some ways, I am still a traditionalist; please allow me to bless the food."

I put my fork down and lowered my head, hoping it would be a short blessing. The prayer was quick, concise, and to the point. When he concluded, I gratefully dug into the salad and began eating. The various flavors hit my tongue in an edible melody. I closed my eyes, savoring each bite I took, chewing slowly.

Although I had not gone hungry, the last couple of years offered fewer and fewer food choices as food prices skyrocketed into a hyperinflation frenzy. Even our successful gardens offered little variety and only part of the year. Many of us, having stocked up on canned and dry goods, were eating through those rather quickly. We realized that only having stocked up canned and dry food was not enough to carry us through the tough times the United States was experiencing. Many people thought the tough times would be over by now, but people were beginning to realize that the tough times had only just begun. Our Kingdom Coordinator has finally accepted that we are in these challenging times for the long haul.

It is the reason why I am here. Our community needs to catch up in establishing our network and food distribution. KC and Mr. Smith believe there is still enough time to put in a sound food distribution system so our community will not go hungry and stay healthy.

But creating a separate network and distribution system is more than getting access to food. It's getting access to food without having to trade our individual freedoms. With the latest rounds of vaccines, the government didn't make it mandatory for people to get the vaccines. What they did was incentivize the inoculations. The Federal Government provided vouchers allowing food purchases at deeply discounted prices. Some states now require a vaccination card to enter grocery stores, which acts as a membership card. In some states, Walgreens, CVS, and Walmart also demand the card to shop at their stores.

"Continue to tell me about yourself." Said Mr. Smith in between bites of his salad.

He looked at me inquisitively and with a wide grin as he watched me eat. I was reluctant to stop eating but recognized that I needed to slow down. Mr. Smith observed this as well. I put my fork down and began my story.

"As I said before, our family had a farm. Although I was not privy to the finances, I believe our farm was thriving. But then, a couple of years ago, my father got sick at the onset of the latest virus. It happened in the early Spring, just before planting season. Unfortunately, by the time he got sick, our farm had already committed to the seed purchases, and it was too late to get out of the contract.

"My older brother Terry and I did our best. But we were so consumed with my father's illness that we did not adequately protect and secure the seeds before planting. A storm came through the area, and we lost a portion of the seeds when our barn was damaged. We planted what we could, but it was not enough to pay off the farm debt for the year in the long run.

"Anyway, my father was sick and weak for much of the Spring and Summer. Our whole church community was praying for his recovery. And he was recovering, though slowly. Then, our doctor recommended that he get the latest vaccination booster shot. The doctor said getting the booster would help my father's weak immune system. Terry did not want him to get the booster. I now understand that Terry has a strong discerning gift. He knew it would not be good for our dad to get the shot. But our dad got the COVID-19 Vaccine shot and subsequent boosters a few years ago and had no issues. I think he thought it would be the same this time as well. But it wasn't. Within hours after receiving the booster, Dad had trouble breathing. We took him to the hospital, where he was admitted. He died 3 days later."

"I am really sorry you lost your father, Tom." Mr. Smith said with sympathy.

I nodded acknowledgment and continued.

"By harvest time, we only had enough to partially pay off the debt owed. My mother went to the bank for either an extension or to refinance the debt, and the bank told her no. Our family had been with this bank for more than 20 years, and yet in our time of need, they would not help us." I said, remembering the pain of our situation.

"So, my mom put the farm up for sale. Although surviving, most of the other farmers in our area did not have the means to purchase our farm.

"One farmer, a good friend of the family, wanted to purchase the farm to help us out and would have allowed us to remain on the farm and repurchase it one day.

"In fact, he needed our farm to help him comply with the cost of greenhouse emissions compliance so that he could maintain the farm and not have to sell. On paper, he should have qualified to make the purchase. But two banks denied him."

The pressure to monitor and reduce greenhouse gas emissions and the carbon footprint has finally come to the United States. It was not exactly a law, but the compliance process attached itself to the banking system. For a business to conduct a typical transaction with its vendors, it had to supply the bank with compliance papers showing its plan for reducing its greenhouse emissions and carbon footprint. Which can be very burdensome for a small or medium size business, especially a farm.

"There was not much time left before the bank would begin foreclosing proceedings," I continued. "One of the banks that denied my mother and our farmer friend told us about a corporation purchasing farm properties. We did not want to sell, but my mother was left with little choice. She sold, and we moved. She purchased a small homestead outside of the city limits. It's less than an acre of land compared to the 20 acres our family-owned. But at least she was able to make a cash purchase." I paused and looked out the window, remembering the grief and rapid changes our family was forced to make.

"The death of my father and the subsequent move put a strain on our family. Especially my brother Terry. He became angry with everyone; my dad for taking the booster, my mom for letting him, and the bank for not lending us or our family friend the money. Terry believed all of it was orchestrated. My dad's illness, the inoculation, the bank's denial to get our land. He eventually headed to Texas to join their cavalry. He believes there will be fighting and wants to be part of it. We don't hear from him often, and I pray daily for his safety."

I stopped talking. I could feel tears starting to swell up, and I didn't want to cry. I swallowed hard and blinked to keep from crying.

Janet brought our entrees. I was grateful for the interruption. I still needed to finish my salad, so I put it aside to finish later. I dug into my burger with eager anticipation. I closed my eyes again and sighed at the taste of the first bite, thankful that I had something else to divert my attention. Although it has been a while since I ate a hamburger, I don't remember it being as flavorful as this one.

"It's all in the meat and spices," said Mr. Smith looking at me with amusement. "Our cows are grass-fed, and most of the spices come directly from the garden out back. So does your salad."

"This may be the best burger I have ever had! The bread is so fresh and tasty, reminding me of my mom's bread. We had a farm with cattle, and our burgers never tasted this good!"

Mr. Smith laughed and continued eating.

Mr. Smith finished eating before I did. He put his fork down and looked at me.

"You know," he began. "I know many people with similar stories. Too many people, in fact. The last 7 years have taken a toll on this nation and the Church. Many questioned their own faith in God. Some left their congregations. Yet, many more have entered the Kingdom as part of the remnant like you and me. The ones who know Jesus Christ of Nazareth, or Yeshua, as some of my friends would say, as our King and as our Savior. I am really sorry you had to go through what you did. But I am glad you are here."

Just as he finished speaking, Janet came over and asked if we were ready for dessert. I took the last bite of my sandwich and was about to polish off my salad. I was pretty full, but I was not ready to admit it. I was going to stuff in as much food as my stomach could hold.

"You are welcome to take your dessert to-go, and we can come back for it later." Mr. Smith said with a smile, reading my mind about eating all the food in front of me.

"Oh, OK," I said, reluctantly letting go of the idea of stuffing myself. Janet said she would hold our dessert, and we could come back for it. I was wondering where we were going next.

As I finished my salad, a woman of medium build came to our table. She introduced herself as Margie, the General Manager of the restaurant. She asked how we enjoyed our meal and wanted to know if we had any questions.

"I do have a couple of questions," I started, remembering my directive. What is the room off to the right? Is it a bar?"

"Yes, it is a bar, an additional eating area, and a stage used to host musicians and singers. We keep the bar area separate for various reasons. We refer to the room you are in as the 'Family Dining Room'. Alcoholic beverages are not allowed in this room. We sell locally brewed beer and wine in the other dining area, but no hard liquor."

"How do you decide what will be on the menu?" I continued with my questions.

"Every week, we take inventory of what we have in stock and what needs to be harvested in our garden. Then we check the inventory of our co-op and community partners. We do this through a dedicated messaging board on our private co-op intranet where we can see who has what available. The Chef is the one who decides the menu from week to week. Sometimes we have 5 items, like this weekend, and

sometimes it's only 3 items." Margie answered, looking at me to see if I had more questions.

"How, then, do you decide what to charge? What type of payment do you take?"

"That's a good question," said Margie. "I am sure Mr. Smith will go into more detail later. The primary way we accept payment at the restaurant is with our community currency. We find that its value has been more stable than even the United States dollar."

Mr. Smith chimed in, "Our co-op has a currency exchange station, and it's where we keep up with the fluctuation of the currencies around the world."

"Even cryptocurrency?" I asked.

"Yes," said Mr. Smith.

Margie continued, "Most of our community has an app on their phone that we tap to accept payment. The community also has a debit card that some prefer to use."

"What if their account goes negative?" I asked, remembering some not-so-fun times with my own bank account.

"The community currency is designed to allow their account to go negative up to a point." Mr. Smith explained further. "When it happens, the member is now using credit. How much is a complex equation that considers what the member contributes to the community in food and/or service, the anticipation of harvest quantity, and harvest season. We also consider the number of people in their household and a few other factors. The equation gets re-evaluated every quarter, and the 'credit limit' for each community member gets adjusted. A person might end the quarter with a negative balance but start the new quarter with a positive balance or possibly vice-versa. But the latter is rare."

"But I will say this," Mr. Smith continued. "It's not like the traditional credit card. For example, when the card goes into credit mode, the member is only allowed to purchase essential food items. This way, we keep with our fundamental mission...that no one goes hungry. You will see for yourself when we go across the street to the main building. There is a wide variety of items to purchase with our community currency, including food. We are still working through some of the kinks. But the idea is that no one in our community lacks food or suffers from any nutritional deficiencies."

I had no more questions, and I thanked Margie for a wonderful lunch and for answering my questions. We got up to leave, and I said goodbye to Janet, who promised to hold my dessert. We walked across the street to the co-op's main trading area.

The co-op Trading Arena

We crossed a 4-lane road to get to the trading arena. The co-op was located in a strip mall. The largest part of the mall looked like what used to be a small department store like Kohls or even a JC Penney. We walked through the doors. It was a sizable open space with multiple rows of booths selling various fresh foods, canned foods, and everything else. I had imagined it would be like an indoor farmers' market. But it was more like a Bazaar. There was a little bit of everything here…. Art, jewelry, clothing, books, and even furniture. As we walked in, to the right of us, there was a set of windows with what appeared to be tellers helping people exchange money like what you would see at a bank. There was a large open area behind the tellers with rows of desks and chairs filled with people peering at their computer screens.

"This is where a person signs up to be part of the co-op, and you can exchange your regular currency for the community currency." Mr. Smith offered as he observed my inquisitive look. "We also keep track of the traders here; it acts as a clearing house for all the trade that goes on in the arena. They trade with each other just as much as with the general public. I should also note that only the community currency is accepted at the trading booths."

"So, when someone makes a purchase, they tap the merchant's phone?"

"You got it," said Mr. Smith. "The transaction gets recorded, and the merchant account is kept and managed here."

"What if the merchant wants to exchange the community currency for another or even cryptocurrency?" I asked.

"They can do that, too."

"Wow!" I exclaimed, taking it all in. The air was alive with many conversations and various kinds of music though faint, hanging in the background of the discussions. I also noticed a security guard observing us, and we walked over to him.

"Hello, Joe," Mr. Smith offered his hand in greeting.

"Hello, Andrew," said Joe, the security guard. I blinked, hearing Mr. Smith's given name for the first time.

"I would like for you to meet Tom. He's visiting us from another community, hoping to learn about what we do here."

"It's a pleasure." Joe reaches his hand towards me in an offer to shake it. I put my hand in his, and he firmly holds and shakes it. He lingered on the hold for a couple of seconds, then released my hand as he asked me an unexpected question. "You're the youngest son?" Joe asks.

"Yes, how did you know?" He smiles but does not answer the question.

"Nice to meet you." He said to me and then nodded at Mr. Smith and walked away.

"What was that about?" I asked Mr. Smith. "And how did he know I was the youngest son?"

"He probably knows much more than that," said Mr. Smith. "Joe is not just a security guard; he is also a Kingdom Watchman."

"A what?"

"A Kingdom Watchman. He has a very high level of discernment. He not only keeps security in the natural but also in the spiritual realm. It's like he can see into people. So, if someone walks through these doors with evil intent, he and the other Kingdom Watchmen can 'discern' this and stop it before any spiritual or even natural damage is done. We keep this building and our other properties, including the restaurant, covered in prayer. People have received warning dreams and visions of potential sabotage periodically over the last couple of years, and we successfully headed off these evil plans.

"Prayer and intercession are just as important if not more important than the natural planning it takes to pull something like this off." He waved his hand in the air indicating everything in front of us. "But we will talk more in-depth about the Spiritual aspects Sunday, and that discussion will take most of the day.

"Margie, the restaurant's general manager, is also a Watchman." Mr. Smith added. "A Watchman can be a man or a woman."

We started walking through the row of booths in front of us. Some were about 4 feet by 8 feet, but other larger booths were double that size. I could see that most of the vegetable booths were to the left of us, closer to the wall and near a set of double doors for the merchants to bring in their produce. The aisle we were walking down included a variety of items. Many were selling home-canned fruits and vegetables. There was even a booth dedicated to selling baby food. The fruits and vegetables were in glass containers of various sizes. Some booths had loafed bread and other bakery items. We passed a couple of booths that had either large coolers or their own refrigerators. Some were selling meat, and others prepared foods. One booth had prepared Mexican cuisine. The one next door sold Asian dishes. There was one on the other side that sold Indian cuisine. A little further down, I could see booths for Middle Eastern, African, and traditional Native American foods.

"With so many restaurants closing, the prepared foods fill that void. The merchants with prepared food do very well here, and many used to own or manage restaurants," Mr. Smith explained.

Mr. Smith continued. "By state law, we are considered a Farmers Market. And since many of our vendors used to own restaurants, they were allowed to maintain their credentials for selling temperature-controlled food. The others, like those selling baked goods or non-temperature-controlled foods like vegetables, comply with our state's Food Act which allows them to sell the foods prepared from their kitchens."

"We use the expertise of our former restaurant owners to help minimize food waste and to help with our plans that no one in our community lacks basic nutrition. The nutritional aspect of food is fundamental when we make plans. What we found is that some people who stored up on food, although not necessarily hungry, we're still nutritionally deficient. We have taken a more holistic approach to our planning. Our co-op is still young, but it's thriving.

More and more people are interested in becoming a part of our vision."

"This is fantastic. There is so much diversity here, but it seems to work. But it also seems complicated. Was it hard to get started?" I asked.

"Well," Mr. Smith began. "That is a story all by itself. Let's sit over here, and I will tell you all about it."

He led us to a small area of tables and chairs. A few people were sitting, some alone, eating what appeared to be the food from the aisle we had just passed. I sat down while Mr. Smith walked to a booth selling water, juices, and homemade sodas. He brought me apple juice at my request. He sat down and then began to tell me how he started on this path.

From the Beginning

"I was getting prophetic words about the future regarding food, finances, and the overall trajectory of the United States economy for about 20 years. Many prophets were. But because I was only seeing a piece of what was coming, I was not sure what to do with what I was receiving...at least not at first. 1 Corinthians Chapter 13 of the Bible speaks about seeing only in part. After talking with others who also saw the future, I slowly began to put together what the future would look like. Then one day, about a year or two before the pandemic, I woke up and heard the word, 'Prepare.' So, I started praying about what that meant. To make a long story short, I felt I was supposed to help the Body of Christ prepare for the food shortage. A daunting task, to say the least!"

Mr. Smith sighed, looking away at nothing in particular.

"Getting started was an uphill battle," he continued. "Doing something like what you see over the weekend takes all of us, not just one or two people. The first part of the battle was talking and convincing church leadership, starting with my church. Most of the people I spoke with did not believe things would get as bad as I believe the Lord showed me at the time. And those who did thought it would only be for a short time.

"Then the pandemic came, and the whole world shut down. Church leadership was willing to at least listen. However, after the initial weeks when people were panicking, food was readily available again, and the sense of urgency was gone.

"I was getting frustrated, not knowing what to do. I had been stocking up on food, and my wife and I started a garden in our yard. We had time to grow and cultivate it during the pandemic. My wife, Judith, began teaching herself how to can some of our grown blueberries, strawberries, and tomatoes. To test things out, we decided to eat off the land, not using grocery stores for 2 months to see how it would go."

Mr. Smith shifted in his seat as he continued.

"Our two teenage children were not on board with this plan, as you can imagine. It meant limited junk food, no Pizza Hut, no McDonald's, etc. But we stocked up on some of their favorite items. We partnered with a farmer friend for our eggs and poultry, and we also purchased a half cow to store in our freezer.

"We chose the months of September and October and gave ourselves a one-month running start. In August that year, we tried to anticipate every food requirement and purchased accordingly. Come September 1st, no restaurants, fast food, or grocery store runs. The only purchase we allowed ourselves was the eggs and poultry.

"The first couple of weeks went well, aside from the occasional complaining of the kids. My wife and I tasked them with preparing their own school lunches, and they were also responsible for one meal a piece during the week."

"Really?!" I exclaimed. "My mother always did the cooking. I could make sandwiches, fix cereal, and scramble eggs, but that was about it. Over the years, I have learned how to prepare some basic meals. But that came later after we moved."

"We believe cooking is a life skill that everyone should have." Mr. Smith replied. "We had forgotten that over the years as life got busy, and we just did what was easy. But the pandemic brought some things back into perspective for us. We used the opportunity to ensure our son and daughter had the life skills to care for themselves. My daughter, Jenna, did help her mother with canning, and my son helped in the garden.

"The first week went well," Mr. Smith resumed.

"The second week also went pretty well. But we discovered we were running low on some spices Judith, my wife, likes to use for cooking. She likes the blends that you find in the grocery store. So, she got creative and started blending her spices with what we had in the house and in the garden. We were also growing Rosemary and Oregano. Judith discovered she enjoyed mixing spices. However, there were some spices, like fresh ginger and garlic, that we did not have access to, and we ran out after about a month.

"Our cheese stock also diminished considerably. We stocked up on dried milk for cooking and discovered we did not have enough. We also had to ration our cooking oils. Although we consulted with people who had homesteads about how much food we would need, our calculations of what we used were off somewhat. We didn't realize how much of these items we needed until we shut down our access to them. On the other hand, we had more than enough salt and pepper and rice and beans." Mr. Smith smiled at the remembrance.

"We were all journaling our experiences daily to have a record of our experience, and Judith and I thought it was just as important to record our emotional journey through this as well. We also wanted to teach our children to do this.

"One thing I noticed about myself during this time is that I had more energy. I didn't actually realize that I lacked any of it before. But I noticed that I slept better and was more alert when I woke up. I didn't need a cup of coffee to do this anymore, although I still had a cup out of habit. I also noticed that my muscles were not as stiff. I attributed these symptoms to getting older. I also lost about 10 pounds. Judith lost weight as well. She was able to come off the blood pressure and cholesterol medication she was taking. We were both more energized and felt better overall.

"There was also a notable difference in the kids. After the first couple of weeks, their moods were more stable and less argumentative. After the first month, they were both excited about preparing and cooking the meal on their assigned day. There was a light competitiveness about who could prepare the most creative and tasty meal. Judith and I enjoyed seeing this side of our children. Since sugary items were limited, both of their faces cleared of acne, and they were less sluggish in the morning.

"Happy with the results thus far, I wanted to know why we were feeling better and seemingly healthier. On the surface, I believed it was because we were no longer eating out and eating less junk food. But I thought that I needed to dig a little further into it. So, I started doing nutrition research. I discovered that we were eating the nutritional properties our bodies needed for optimum health!

"This was an amazing discovery since we randomly chose what to grow in our garden and what to stockpile. Of course, we had a basic idea. But my research discovered essential vitamins and mineral properties in the foods we eat that our body needs to function properly. Our health issues resulted from not consistently having enough of these specific nutrients in our diet. I learned about trace minerals and how they play an important role in our overall health. The revelation hit me like a lightning bolt. God wants us to live in divine health! I knew then that the nutritional component had to be foundational for whatever we did moving forward."

"What are trace minerals?" I asked.

Mr. Smith picked up his phone and pulled up a list. "Iron, chromium, copper, zinc, iodine, manganese, potassium, magnesium, and selenium. There are more, but what I just mentioned are the most recognized."

My eyes grew wide as I listened to what he was saying. It never occurred to me to be concerned about minerals, not to mention trace minerals, and I had no idea how important they were. I did know of people who 'cured' themselves of physical ailments through food. But even now, that was becoming difficult because the food choices were drying up rapidly due to low supply and increased cost.

"I also believe God wanted me to start with our family so I could gain some practical knowledge," Mr. Smith continued.

"One thing this experiment taught me was that a change in eating and our overall food habits in this country would not be easy. Even in our process, we knew we would be in food isolation for two months and prepared for it. But we also knew that we could and would return to purchasing groceries when it was over. Nevertheless, it was a start.

"I didn't realize how dependent we as a society had become

on our normal routine of going to the grocery store, eating out for our food needs, and of course, our wants. And not just for working folks. Even less fortunate people have access to food in our country, although not always nutritious.

"I asked the Lord, was this it? What is it that you want me to communicate? *'Prepare,'* is what I heard again. I kept seeking Him for clarity and direction.

"To summarize, through prayer and fasting, I was made to see Heaven's point of view on what we were to prepare for and how we were to prepare. My family's experiment was part of the process of Him revealing the blueprint, but there was much more to it. He wanted us, His Body, to do more to be ready for the coming changes.

"What you have seen so far is only part of the blueprint; and not even the first part. The largest hurdle and the greatest learning curve is still yet to come."

Mr. Smith paused and took a deep sip of his water.

"Is it the blueprint you are showing me this weekend?" I asked.

"What you take home with you will only be a partial blueprint. The plan also includes finances, housing, medical, insurance.... every part of the economic system we have taken for granted for several generations. Our country is going through a metamorphosis. As the Body in our current age, we have the unique position of deciding the outcome of the changes we are witnessing in our country.

"I understood that we had to prepare a safety net. So that we would not be in crisis mode as the changes come but rather in a position of strength and authority. A position similar to Joseph as described in Genesis 41. Do you know the story?"

"Yes, I do," I replied. "Joseph received a revelation of Pharaoh's dream and was made to oversee stocking up grain for the coming famine as foretold in the dream."

Mr. Smith nodded approval. "I encourage you to go back and read again, including the subsequent chapters. There is a lot packed into the story, and the strategies are woven into what we are doing."

"OK," I said, planning in my mind to re-read that portion of Genesis before I go to bed tonight.

"You did by choice what many people are experiencing now... lack of access to grocery stores and restaurants," I said. "Only now, it's not a choice. There are tons of people who don't like what is happening with their choices being taken away.

"It's been stressful for many of us because we don't want to depend on the government for our needs, and we feel the price is too high. But we have seen some people comply with government requirements to keep from going hungry and continue having access to medical and housing. Some didn't want to but felt they had no choice.

"I think the biggest reason why many Americans didn't plan is that we all felt that the problems were short-lived and things would go back to normal...pre-COVID normal at the very least. The United States has had its share of recessions and inflation. But we've always recovered in the past. This time it's different." My voice trailed off as I contemplated what I had just said.

"Are you aware of the Patriot Act?" Mr. Smith asked me.

"No, I don't believe so," I answered.

"The Patriot Act was passed into law right after the 9/11 tragedy in 2001. It was sold as a law that would help keep our country safe from future terrorist attacks. In reality, the law paved the way for some of the civil liberties promised to us in the Constitution to slowly erode. Like our privacy, for example. The Patriot Act allows the government to monitor email and web browsing if they suspect a terrorist connection. The problem with the law's wording is that it broadens the definition of who could be a terrorist suspect contradicting the 3rd and 4th Amendments to the Constitution.

"Then came COVID-19. We saw mass shutdowns mandated by the Federal and local governments. Only those businesses deemed essential were allowed to remain open. What is considered essential can be very subjective. In some states, churches were considered non-essential. And for the most part, we, the church, agreed and closed our doors.

"Then the next President of the United States mandated vaccinations for government and other essential workers. You must understand, Tom, I am not against keeping the public safe from danger. But if you followed the science of the virus from beginning to end and researched successful treatments, what the government was trying to do at that time did not make sense in the face of logic. There was so much fear-based information pushed out by the media that most people failed to see the truth of what was actually happening. It was like the whole world was in a petri dish, and someone wanted to see how far they could go with these mandates.

"The unfortunate result is that a large portion of the population reacted like sheep and complied with what many believed to be unconstitutional mandates. I am saying this to point out that the enemy has prepared us for this kind of world for a long time. We generally did not have the eyes to see what was happening. And now that many do see, it's almost too late."

"Anyway, we veered off topic a bit." Mr. Smith continued finishing his water. "Would you like to take a break?" He asked.

"Yes, if you don't mind," I said gratefully.

"OK. I will get us some more drinks. The restrooms are a little further back to the right." Mr. Smith offered as he got up to get us more water and apple juice. I went in the direction I was instructed.

When I returned, Mr. Smith then went to the restroom. I took the opportunity to look around. There was a lot of activity, and the tables where we were sitting were now all occupied. I could smell bakery goods in one direction and Ethic foods in another. I looked up at the ceiling. There were multiple ceiling fans spinning slowly, circulating the air. People of all different ages, backgrounds, and ethnicity were walking through the aisles. Many were pushing grocery carts filled with various items. Some had their own bags. I saw a few with the Co-op logo.

Mr. Smith returned, sat down, took a sip of his water, and resumed talking.

"Let's see, where was I…oh yes. I kept some church leaders informed of what my family was doing. There were a few people who were curious about it. I am not a social media person, but my kids… after they stopped complaining…decided to do their journaling via social media. To my surprise, they had just over fifteen thousand followers by the end of the two months! A few were their friends and members of our church. These young people began to speak with their parents about what we were doing.

"The following months after our personal journey with food and nutrition, we had several families who had questions about getting started. But the church leadership was still not on board."

Frowning, Mr. Smith looked down at his water.

"So," His head popped up, and he smiled at me mischievously. "I decided to do something completely out of character."

"What do you mean?" I asked.

"I am usually a follow-the-rules kind of guy. Meaning I believed in church hierarchy and submitting to leadership. But I woke up one morning, and the Holy Spirit was very heavy in the bedroom. I looked over, and Judith was still asleep. I felt an overwhelming peace come over me. I felt a strong impression of someone in the room with me. Then a scripture popped into my head, Ephesians 1:18-23." He opened his phone to pull up the scripture. "I am going to read this to you in the amplified:

> 'By having the eyes of your heart flooded with light, so that you can know and understand the hope to which He has called you, and how rich is His glorious inheritance in the saints (His set-apart ones), and [so that you can know and understand] what is the immeasurable and unlimited and surpassing greatness of His power in and for us who believe, as demonstrated in the working of His mighty strength, which He exerted in Christ

when He raised Him from the dead and seated Him and His [own] right hand in the heavenly [places], far above all rule and authority and power and dominion and every name that is named [above every title that can be conferred], not only in this age and in this world, but also in the age and the world which are to come. And He has put all things under His feet and appointed Him the universal and supreme Head of the Church [a headship exercised throughout the church]. Which is His body, the fullness of Him Who fills all in all [for in that body lives the full measure of Him Who makes everything complete and Who fills everything everywhere with Himself.]'

Mr. Smith continued. "When I read this, I understood what I had to do and how to move forward. So much revelation dropped into my Spirit all at once that I had to catch my breath!" He looked at me and could see the confusion on my face.

"Let me unpack this for you." He continued. "In a nutshell, this scripture first pointed to my calling, second declared that Christ's authority, power, and dominion are above every name and title. This means that Christ is the head, and not anyone else on earth or in Heaven can take His place. I was given a directive and purpose, and I allowed natural men to tell me not to do it!"

"You went against your church leadership?" I asked, surprised.

"I did. Not because I wanted to but because I realized that I ultimately answered to Jesus. But I didn't sneak. I let them know exactly what I was going to do."

"How did they react?"

"Not well." Mr. Smith frowned again. "But all is well now. Please understand I am not saying to not submit to your leadership. That is not the message here. A difference of opinion is not enough to rebel. This was much more than that. When I had the encounter in the bedroom, I saw what would happen if I did not obey Christ.

The encounter also served as a confirmation for me. Sometimes we need those when man does not see what we see. The encounter served as a witness as well as a revelation."

I nodded in understanding and was relieved that his situation had ended well.

"What did you do next?" I asked.

"Well," he continued. "My wife and I talked, and we made a radical plan.

The Call-to-Action Tent Meeting

"We purchased organic seeds, which generally grow well in our area. We chose multiple herbs, 2 varieties of tomatoes, carrots, strawberries, blueberries, lettuce, greens, kale, squash, beets, corn, and peas. We partnered with a friend who could supply soil, and then we purchased large quantities and various sizes of plant containers. We rented a storage room to hold the containers and seeds. Then we planned an old-fashioned tent meeting," Mr. Andrew explained.

"We set a date and prayed and prayed that the weather would cooperate, which it did. We put the word out on our children's social media and through word of mouth. We had a lot of help. Once we got things started, volunteers came forward, many of whom had their own gardens, which was helpful because they had knowledge about growing in our area.

"When the day came, I was surprised at how many people showed up. The tent we rented could hold about 100 people, and more than twice that amount showed up. People came with their own chairs and sat outside the tent. Some stood. We were in a park, so others were a little further off, sitting under trees. But they were all there to hear what I had to say."

"Were you nervous?" I asked, wide-eyed at the story.

"I was." Mr. Smith admitted. "But I was determined to move forward. I am not a preacher, and I hadn't done a lot of public speaking…at least not to a crowd as large as was there. I spoke from the heart on what I was shown. I shared our family experience, and I also had my children share their experiences as well. I wanted people to understand that we understood how much of a change this would be; the time and learning curve involved.

"Instead of sending them away with information, I did a call to action. We had tables set up with the seeds and containers, and there were also three pick-up trucks loaded with soil. The gardeners were stationed at the seed tables to offer advice, answer questions, and take their information. We offered people free seeds and containers to start their own gardens."

"Wow! You must have had a rush of people take you up on your offer!" I exclaimed.

"We did." Mr. Smith said with a smile. "The response was overwhelming."

"How could you afford to do that? That must have cost a lot of money. The tent and chairs, and not to mention the seeds, containers, and even the dirt."

"Well, the dirt was free. But not the seeds and containers and, indeed, not the tent or the park rental. It was an investment, to be sure, but worth every penny. At my wife's insistence, we put out a couple of donation containers. We didn't solicit, just had the containers in view if people wanted to donate. We took in about a third of the cost.

"I mentioned that the volunteers were getting everyone's information?"

"Yes, you did," I said, taking a mental note.

"That was the beginning of our community. We created our own Intranet and established a database to use for communication. The first thing we did was send out emails thanking them for their attendance and encouraging communication regarding how their plants were growing. We eventually developed an encrypted application for the iPhone and Android that's linked to our Intranet. It's the primary way we communicate today.

"Many people expressed their desire to take the next steps." Mr. Smith continued. "There were also people who wanted to create a garden, but because of space, physical limitations, or time constraints, they didn't feel they could. But we had our community. Now it was time to get organized.

"I got a call the next day from the head of another local church in the area. He and his wife wanted to partner with us to establish a community and our own food distribution network. He offered his church location for meetings.

"We had our first meeting for people interested in doing more.

We established committees for various topics; planting the right vegetables for optimum nutrition, soil health, planting seasons for our area, website design, logistics, and communication, to name a few. In a nutshell, that's how we got started."

"I am curious," I began my question. "What would you have done if another church had not offered to partner with you?"

"To be sure, partnering with the other church helped us to move forward faster and with a financial cushion in place. But we planned to push forward regardless. The community and network would have been smaller and possibly would have grown at a slower pace. The donations we received were the beginning of our community budget, and that would have happened either way. Judith and I were already on track to ensure our family was taken care of if everything else failed. But we had faith that our efforts would be successful in the long run...and they were."

"I was thinking about our little community back home and where we go from here," I said.

Mr. Smith nodded and began to explain. "Many smaller communities in this region and around the country have had successful beginnings. We are networked with many of them. You don't have to be a big community to be successful. Your community will have to determine what success looks like for them. We have determined success by how well we can provide our community's nutritional needs. We will talk tomorrow about how that works."

As Mr. Smith finished talking, he looked up and around, and I did the same. The tables where we were sitting were empty, some booths were closing down, and there were fewer people moving about. I looked at my watch, shocked at how much time had passed.

"I'd better get you to Susie's." He said, getting up from his seat.

I recognized the name. She is hosting me at her home while I am here. Mr. Smith pulled out his phone and began texting.

We got up, proceeded to the front, and then crossed the street back to the Co-op restaurant where we had parked. Now, the parking lot was completely full. We walked in, and all the tables were full, and I could hear music coming from the other room. Janet was still there. She brought us our dessert, and we headed to the car.

"Susie lives about 20 minutes away." Mr. Smith offered. I nodded, and we drove away.

When we got there, Susie was waiting for us at the door, and she greeted us both and invited us in. Mr. Smith declined the invitation and said he had to get home but would pick me up tomorrow around 10 a.m. We said our goodbyes, and I followed Susie into her home.

"Oh, Wow!" I exclaimed. "This looks like something you would see in a fairytale!"

"Susie lived in a ranch-style home with an open floor plan. There were plants lined up on every wall and throughout the living area. The tables in between the chairs had flowering plants, and you could also see walls of plants in the kitchen.

"Let me show you around." Susie offered.

To the right was a dining area that was turned into a botanical garden of sorts. There were two rows of shelving with plant lighting and lemon and lime trees growing in large pots.

"You've brought the outside indoors," I observed.

Susie laughed. "Yes, I guess I did. I wanted to have a variety of eatable plants, and not everything grows well in our climate."

Susie showed me the kitchen. There were mainly herbs growing, and I recognized most of them. She opened the patio door, and we walked out. Susie did have a sitting area but also plants lining the railings. Some stairs went into the backyard. Here she had rows of containers with various plants growing. Most were mature, considering the time of year, and some containers were empty.

"The empty containers were already harvested, and I will be planting the fall crop in a couple of weeks," Susie said, observing where my gaze went.

"What did you do with your harvest?" I asked. "Did you can? Store? Or did you sell what you grew?"

"All of the above. It's just me now. No husband and the kids have moved away. So, I determine my needs plus a little extra for guests like you. I share a booth at the co-op with a neighbor, and we sell some. Another neighbor down the street has chickens, and she brings me eggs and the occasional chicken, and I let her 'shop' my garden. I also trade for other items like meat, rice, flour, and sugar."

We went back inside. Susie took me down the hall and showed me the hall bath I will be using and my room. I put my bag on the bed and followed her back out.

"Are you hungry?" She asked.

"Just a little. We had a big lunch."

"How about a sandwich? Or maybe some soup?" She smiled. "I can offer you a chicken sandwich and/or beef vegetable soup."

"I still have my dessert. Can I just have the sandwich?" I ask.

"Of course. Coming right up."

Susie prepared the sandwich, asking me what toppings I would like. She had everything, including onions, all grown in her garden. I ate my sandwich, then my dessert.

She offered me a cup of herbal tea, and we talked a little more, and I told her about my background. We said goodnight, and I took a second cup of tea to my room, sat at the desk, and began to recall all that had happened.

I began writing notes with all the details I could remember. I was explicitly told not to voice record anything in case I lost my phone or it was confiscated on the way back home. I thought it was a little paranoid that anyone would be interested in tapping my phone or even taking it. But we were living in bizarre times, and my state was becoming more like a totalitarian state every day.

I brought a large business journal with me and began writing down what Mr. Smith had told me earlier in the day. I also wrote down questions I wanted to ask him. But I suspected the questions would be answered in the next two days without asking. Writing everything down took almost two hours.

My eyelids were getting heavy. It had been a long couple of days traveling and then an informative and interesting day with Mr. Smith. I was excited and satisfied with the visit so far, but I was also exhausted and glad that we were not meeting until 10 a.m. the following day. I was planning on sleeping in. Eager to read the story of Joseph from a different perspective, I opened up the Book of Genesis on my phone Bible App. I couldn't keep my eyes open, so I decided to read it in the morning after I showered. I got ready for bed and turned out the light. It was barely 10 p.m., but it felt like midnight. I drifted off to sleep thinking about my brother.

DAY 2

Breakfast

*T*HE SUN SHONE BRIGHTLY THROUGH the blinds when I opened my eyes the following day; my window was obviously facing east. I looked at my watch; 6:59 a.m. I slept longer than usual. Being a farmer's son, I was used to getting up around 5 a.m. I showered, shaved, dressed, and opened my Bible app to Genesis.

I picked up on something I had not noticed before. Joseph did not give away grain. He sold it. He not only sold it to foreigners but also to the Egyptians. Joseph arranged for the grain to be stored up and available…. but not for free. The Egyptians gave up first their money, then their livestock, and then their land so that they could eat. What happened was a wealth transfer from the landowners to Pharoah. The farmers were allowed to stay on farms, but from the time they sold their land, they farmed for Pharoah.

I was pondering this revelation when there was a knock on my door. It was Susie asking if I wanted breakfast. I was hungry, so I came out of my room and followed her to the kitchen. Susie had prepared scrambled eggs with cheese, potatoes, and chicken sausages. Some toast just popped up from the toaster and on the table was butter and homemade strawberry jam. Also, a glass of apple juice and a glass of water.

"Have a seat," Susie instructed.

I sat down. Susie put the plate of food in front of me, and I began eating. Then I remembered that I did not say grace. My fork stopped halfway to my mouth.

"Oops," I said. "I forgot to say grace."

Susie laughed. "I'm sure the Lord knows you're grateful. I don't stand on ceremony much."

I said a quick grace under my breath and then put the fork into my mouth. Susie sat down on the opposite side of the table and began eating.

"How is it?" She asked.

"Delicious. The flavors are so vibrant and wonderful."

Halfway through finishing my breakfast, I asked Susie questions about her botanical home and what she was growing. She told me some stories about some of the plant life and the learning curve she went through to get to this point.

"Susie, how did you and Mr. Smith meet?

"You mean Andrew?" Susie asked.

"Yes," I replied. Remembering that I heard Mr. Smith's first name yesterday at the Co-op.

"We met at the first tent meeting. I was inspired by Andrew's speech and so inspired by his family that I wanted more information about his plans. I had just retired from my job, still learning how to live on a fixed income. The tent meeting was right on time as I was trying to figure out how to save money and was seriously thinking about growing my own food but not quite sure where to start. I believe that the tent meeting was anointed by God!

"They provided seeds, pots, and soil. I took two kinds of seeds, lettuce and cucumber; I love salads. Anyway, soon after, they started having meetings and offered various classes on gardening. I didn't miss not one class. I participated in every class they offered, hungry to learn about gardening. They also taught us about the nutritional needs for every stage of life and helped us plan our gardens accordingly.

"Over time, the classes varied to include how to get optimum nutrition with a partial garden, bartering on a budget, trading your skills for food, creative housing, and a lot of other classes. They really tried to cover every aspect of the American lifestyle and how to transition to self-sufficiency.

"Eventually, I started harvesting my own seeds." She continued. "So now I don't have to purchase seeds anymore.

"I realized from Andrew's speech in the tent meeting how dependent we all were on the systems that were set up for us. Not to say they were bad. But when we moved from agricultural to industrial in the western world, systems were set up to accommodate larger populations in our cities and towns. These processes were not wrong. But people became dependent on the infrastructures and forgot how to take care of themselves. We relied on city infrastructure for our utilities, garbage disposal, and other necessities. We became dependent on grocery stores and restaurants to feed us. We even got to where food and other essentials, including groceries, could be delivered to our homes with a few clicks on our phones or computers.

"Don't get me wrong, I loved the conveniences and used all of them! Especially during COVID. I started ordering my groceries online like many people, and I used delivery services when I wanted food from my favorite restaurant."

"Yes, me too." I offered. "I think I miss pizza delivery the most. It was quick and easy. But even towards the end, ordering pizza was becoming too expensive, and the pizza quality was awful. I don't really like to cook, so I was definitely into fast food and pizza. I got a job working at a restaurant after we sold the farm. Figured that was the best way to get a free meal and some decent food."

Susie nodded and continued. "Taking the classes helped me to understand my nutritional requirements, how to keep the soil healthy, and choose the foods that offered specific nutrients my body required for optimum health. With guidance, I developed a plan for myself. But I discovered that if I only grew food outside during the warmer months, I would not necessarily get all of the nutritional benefits during the winter months. We had many meetings talking this through and came up with various options for people knowing that every situation would be different. I began studying hydroponics and aeroponics. I tried both. So, what you see is a combination based on what works well for me. But remember I told you that I began harvesting my own seeds?"

"Yes, I remember," I replied.

"I had to learn how to harvest seeds for the garden and also for hydro and aeroponics. It was a learning curve…." Susie paused, seemingly deep in thought.

Just as Susie stopped talking, the doorbell rang, and Susie got up to answer it. It was Mr. Smith and another gentleman. He looked like Mr. Smith, the same height, same build, only much younger.

"Well, hello there!" Susie exclaimed, referring to them both but looking at the younger man. "I was not expecting two tall and handsome men!" She stepped to the left, letting them enter.

"I brought Andy. I thought Tom would appreciate someone closer to his age tagging along. Also, I have a meeting later, so Andy will take over for me." Mr. Smith explained.

They walked over to the kitchen table, where Susie made introductions. Andy was Mr. Smith's son, who looked about 20 or 21, around two or three years younger than me. We all sat down at the kitchen table as Susie recounted our conversation to them.

"Very good." Mr. Smith said when Susie was finished. He then looked at me.

"You have an interview at the restaurant this morning. Eleven, I believe?" He asked.

"Oh, I almost forgot about that. Yes, 11:00," I replied.

The interview was my cover story in case I needed one. The state where I live instituted customs checkpoints upon entry into the state. Checkpoints were set up in the airports, bus and train stations, and main highways. Their reason was to stop drug trafficking, sex trafficking, illegal aliens, and gun smuggling. All guns were made illegal for everyone except law enforcement by the state legislature due to the increase in mass shootings. A gun license from another state was no longer honored. At best, the guns were confiscated. At worst, it meant jail time. Every person entering and leaving the state was logged into a database. The officers at the checkpoints had the authority to search the person and/or the vehicle and ask any question about an individual's whereabouts. A person could be detained if the officer was suspicious of the answers or how they presented themselves.

There were stories about their profiling methods. A friend of a friend greeted the officer with a blessing and was searched, questioned, and detained for 24 hours. Another person I heard about had the star of David hanging from their rearview mirror, and he was also searched and detained. A Muslim family whose son worked at the same restaurant where I worked were all detained returning from a funeral. They had the funeral program as proof, but that didn't matter. The only reason they knew they were Muslim was that the mother and daughter wore a hijab. The reason given for the searches was suspicion of terrorist activity. More and more, the investigations were happening to people.

"Before we go, I want to talk with you about the plan and its phases." Mr. Smith continued.

I went to get my notebook, and Susie cleared off the table. We all settled around the table with our drinks when I got back. Mr. Smith, Andy, and I had glasses of water, and Susie sat down with a cup of herbal tea.

The 3-Part Plan

"The first step, what we call **Tier 1**," Mr. Smith began. "Starts with the individual or family unit. It's the self-sufficiency stage. The Co-op offers ongoing in-person classes. We also offer video conferencing and video replays, and we can also offer one-on-one coaching as needed."

"Tier 1 begins with an assessment of where the individual or family unit is currently in terms of self-sufficiency. For now, we will mainly concern ourselves with food security and nutrition. But other areas sometimes need to be addressed, like housing and employment. These areas are often connected, and we do have safety nets in place. But ultimately, the goal is to help activate a plan for food self-sufficiency."

The first part of Tier 1 is determining the nutritional need and quantities for the individual or family. Based on our research, we understand the essential nutrition needed depending on what stage of life a person is in. We also have quantified information for food based on physical ailments, diseases, and disabilities.

"We then teach them about the fruits, vegetables, and herbs that grow well in this area using the USDA growing zone map as well as farmers and gardeners who have experience growing in this region. With this information, combined with the family or individual's preferences, we can help them develop a basic plan for their food nutrition.

"We understand that someone working full-time outside the home will not have much time or energy to devote to a full garden. But perhaps they want to grow one or two items. Or, perhaps the garden responsibility can be given to the older children or another adult in the home."

"What do you do when you run across someone unwilling or unable to grow anything?" I ask.

"We have options for that as well. But this is our lowest level of self-sufficiency. That being said, these plans have a successful track record, and they are working." Mr. Smith answered.

"Can you give an example of this?" I ask, taking notes.

"I can." Susie jumped in. "My next-door neighbor, Tammy. She works a lot of hours and does not have much time or energy to maintain a garden, but she is definitely on board with the concept. She's not really a cook either, except for basic meals on the weekends. Since I bake bread and make my own jam, she gets her bread and jam from me. Eggs we both get from our neighbor down the street. Tammy goes to the co-op and purchases her prepared meals weekly. She pops them in the oven or microwave when she gets home from work. On the weeks when she is out of town, I purchase prepared food for her. I also supplement some of her meals when I cook. Tammy is part of the co-op, so she exchanges the U.S. dollar for the co-op currency and then transfers the agreed-upon amount to my account."

"My friend's uncle has an extra bedroom in his home," Andy said, offering another example. "He is too busy with his job, but he is totally a believer in my dad's vision. In exchange for room and board, his boarder, who also happens to be a student at the University, tends his garden. He grows enough food for them both."

"Some other friends of mine, a couple," Susie chimed in again, "They are busy people also and used to eat out a lot. They weren't sure how to make the adjustment, and frankly, they were reluctant because they liked their lifestyle the way it was. We've run into a lot of that, haven't we, Andrew?"

Mr. Smith nodded in agreement.

"Anyway, when I went for a visit, I found that they had rhubarb growing in their backyard. I knew of a person who used rhubarb in many of her baking recipes, and I got them together. As a result, she went and harvested their rhubarb. Since they were both a part of the co-op, the couple got credit for the rhubarb harvested from their yard, and Patty, my baker friend, also benefited from providing prepared and canned rhubarb to the co-op.

"Well, the couple got excited about the exchange and expanded their rhubarb stalks into a larger garden. All they grow is rhubarb. Their garden takes care of 50% of their food needs which they use to purchase prepared foods weekly. For now, they are satisfied with this as they both still work outside of the home."

"We pride ourselves on creative solutions based on the needs of our members, and we don't bind them in a one-size-fits-all process." Mr. Smith said. "That being said, our goal is for everyone to have a garden and/or access to fresh food, meat, eggs, and other locally grown products."

"**Tier 2** has to do with our connections to farms," Mr. Smith took a sip from his glass of water and continued. "Most of the farmers that are part of our co-op are local small and medium size farms who were pushed out of the supply chain because they could not handle the compliance burden. The process of cataloging their Emissions and offering a viable solution for their carbon footprint was too much for them.

"The SEC…that is, the Securities and Exchange Commission requires publicly traded companies to disclose their greenhouse gas emissions direct and indirect impact on the environment. Although small and medium size farms are not publicly traded, a large part of the supply chain that they sell to includes publicly traded companies. So, the requirement would apply to them as well.

"However, I will say that our farming partners are very low carbon and emissions contributors. It's the burdensome compliance procedures that knocked them out of the game. The continuous measuring of emissions increased their fragile farming operations' administrative, labor, and legal costs. American farmers were already dealing with drought or flooding, depending on where the farm was located. They were also dealing with increased fertilizer costs and increases in gas prices and other supplies. Their harvest yields were lower as a result. This would generally cause a price increase to compensate for the lower yields. Because the problem has been persistent and not getting any better over the last several years, the price increases have not been enough to compensate for the lower harvest yields.

"We saw this as an opportunity to help the farmers and the co-op so that we already had an alternative when the food supply started to dry up. As a result, even the price of meat and other commodities began to stabilize within our community when the conventional grocery store prices were skyrocketing."

"We have cattle farms, chicken farms, beekeepers, apple orchards, maple tree groves, hops, barley, corn, and wheat, to name a few. We believe our 'farm-to-table' model is suitable for everyone and also good for our planet. The farm-to-table approach also reduces waste and minimizes the time it takes for the product to get to the consumer. The reduced time alone increases the nutritional value of fruits and vegetables since the nutrients begin to degrade once they are removed from the earth."

Mr. Smith paused to look at me.

I began speaking, "I hope we haven't missed our opportunity to connect with the farmers in our area."

I was thinking about how our farmer friend was forced to sign an exclusive contract with a larger corporate farm.

I continued, "The farms that could comply with the emissions and carbon mandates signed contracts with the more giant corporations that forbade them from selling independently. Many pulled out of locally owned grocery stores, farmers' markets, and local co-ops because of their contract obligations.

"Also, many smaller farms sold to the larger farm corporations because they could not comply with the environmental requirements. Our food supply is not only costly, but it is also slowly shrinking. Which is why I am here, to learn how you all do things."

"That brings us to **Tier 3**," Mr. Smith said.

"Tier 3 is trading with other states and countries. Our network is growing, and in our area, we are on track to sell what we grow here to other regions of the United States and North America in the next year or two. We are working on the logistics for this as we speak.

"However, how the vote goes this fall for the President and some of the local offices will impact the direction we take as some states will likely close their borders in anticipation of potential conflict.

"We are testing out some of our strategies now. Already, we have seen our products confiscated in two states, and they falsely claimed drug trafficking and kept the food for themselves. Fortunately, our truckers were let go…. a strong indication of their innocence." Mr. Smith frowned and then continued.

"We had better success with trains, and we even flew some cargo to bypass certain states. The flights were successful but, as you can imagine, very expensive due to the fuel costs. We have, at least partially, established a route through a neighboring state using the state's two-lane roads, staying off the main Interstate highway. But we feel it's a matter of time before the state roads are untenable. We are also exploring underground routes, literally and figuratively.

"What we just talked about is a high-level overview. The plan works here because we started early, and our state is less draconian than yours. That being said, I believe we can successfully help you with a plan. But your plan will have to be a little more covert. You will see what I mean on tour today. Actually, you are sitting in an example." Mr. Smith looked around Susie's home with all of its varied plant life.

"Did you expect to see this when I brought you here?" He asked.

"No," I said. "I was taken aback."

"What you see here will be an integral part of your community plan. Part of the strategy is hiding your food supply in plain sight. We will help by supplying you with seeds to start and teach you how to harvest seeds from your crops."

"Cool," I said, nodding and smiling at the prospect of receiving seeds. It has become harder to obtain seeds for growing, organic or otherwise. When we had the farm, we only used GMO or Genetically Modified seeds from our supplier since it was in our contract to purchase their seeds every year. We just thought that was what we had to do. My mom also purchased heirloom seeds every year from a separate online supplier for the garden. Over time, obtaining a variety of seeds had become difficult. The one seed supplier we could still get seeds from recently stopped selling to the public.

Our community had gotten good at reproducing potatoes, garlic, onions, and even lettuce. But because we started late and lacked seed harvesting knowledge, we were behind and did not have enough vegetables and fruits to consistently feed everyone.

On our family farm, we considered ourselves to be self-sufficient. But we now understand that true self-sufficiency is not just in growing the food but the ability to reproduce the same results in quantity and quality year after year. We needed the ability to harvest our own seeds.

"We'd better get going." Mr. Smith said, looking at his watch.

I retrieved my backpack from my room, put the notebook inside, and met Mr. Smith and Andy at the door. We said goodbye to Susie and began walking to the car. I turned to look back at the house and then at the houses on either side. The neighborhood had a uniform look, and there was no distinct difference between the houses next door to Susie's other than subtle color differences on the exterior of the homes. Walking or driving by, a person who didn't know would never suspect that Susie's house was a literal botanical garden on the inside.

We got in the car, I on the passenger side and Andy in the back sitting directly behind me. Mr. Smith started up the car, and we drove away.

"Our first stop will be the restaurant for your interview," Mr. Smith said as he clicked the turn signal to make a left turn. "The restaurant is just down the street, about 10 minutes away."

The Interview

We were on another main street. There were multiple apartment complexes, office parks, and a hospital complex with various medical offices. Also, a few fast-food eating places and a few national sit-down restaurants I recognized were open. The street was more active, with fewer boarded-up buildings. The area had a very familiar feel to it. In fact, it reminded me of one of the suburban business districts back home.

We turned into the parking lot of one of the sit-down restaurants, which was part of the same chain where I worked back home. The interview was supposedly for an assistant manager position.

We all went inside. I didn't expect Mr. Smith and Andy to come inside with me, so I was not sure what was supposed to happen at this point.

Mr. Smith took the lead and requested to see the General Manager. While we waited, we were instructed to sit at a booth towards the back, away from the occupied tables.

Mr. Smith noticed the confused look on my face. "Don't worry," he said. "You will understand what's happening in a few minutes."

Andy nodded in agreement, giving me a reassuring smile.

"OK," I responded. I took a deep breath and sat down next to Andy. Mr. Smith sat opposite; his serene composure different from my anxious one.

A server came over and asked for our drink orders. Being in a nationally owned restaurant, I knew they would have soda, so I ordered Mountain Dew, and Andy ordered a Pepsi. Mr. Smith ordered coffee.

A few minutes passed by, and the server brought our drinks. Shortly after, a man of medium build walked toward us with a cup of coffee in his hand, and he sat down next to Mr. Smith and looked pointedly at me.

I felt as if he was looking straight into my soul, and I was a little uneasy for a split second. But the feeling quickly passed.

"Tom, meet our Senior Watchman, Joshua. He's also the General Manager here." Mr. Smith said.

"Watchman?" I ask. "Oh, you mean…."

"Yep," Mr. Smith replied, anticipating my question. "He's the head Watchman and one of our lead intercessors for our community."

"But you work *here?*" I looked at Joshua with an inquisitive look.

Joshua laughed hardily, still looking at me, studying my expression.

"Yes," Joshua began. "I am more or less the spy in the enemy camp. This area, where the restaurant is located, is in the heart of large corporate businesses and major hospital chains. The spiritual pulse of what is trending for our country can be felt here. When I walk or drive down the street, I pick up a lot, and I then take it back to our intercessory team."

"Joshua is just one of our intercessory leaders. Tomorrow, you will meet with one of the other leaders, Deborah." Mr. Smith offered.

"So…," I began talking, trying to fit the pieces together. "So, I am not actually going to interview you about the assistant manager position?"

Joshua laughed again. "My dear boy, you've been on an interview since you arrived."

I was even more confused.

"Stop teasing him, man." Andy chimed in, grinning.

"What Joshua means," Mr. Smith began. "Is that we needed to vet you spiritually to determine how much information to give you. This is not only for our benefit but for yours as well. Once we have determined you are not on a spy mission of your own, we determine your 'spiritual IQ'."

"Spiritual IQ?" I ask.

"Margie at the restaurant and Joe at the Co-op are strong discerners." Mr. Smith explained, ignoring my question.

"They gave you the green light to continue to move forward. If

Joshua does the same…which I am pretty sure he will…then we will continue with the tour. We are about to show you some of the more sensitive aspects of our operation.

We took this specific approach with you because your community will need to put in similar security measures within the community when you return home. I wanted to give you a taste of what that could look like."

I nodded. "Oh, I think I understand. Nobody suspects you?" I queried.

"Nope," he said. "It also helps that I am the General Manager. The influence and authority of my position allows me to see and act when I discern something amiss either spiritually or in the natural."

"Like what?" I ask.

"Well," Joshua continued. "Just the other day, we had an issue with a new employee. Someone my assistant manager hired. He's clueless on spiritual matters. Anyway, I walked into the dining area just before we were about to open, and this employee was praying over the tables. I thought this was odd, and for a split second, was about to welcome the prayers, but then the room began to feel very dark."

"Dark?"

"Yes, spiritually dark. It was like a dark shadow was cast over the areas that she prayed…or rather cursed, and the darkness spread as she continued."

"What did you do?" I asked wide-eyed, staring at Joshua.

"I told her to stop. She was caught off guard and gave some excuse that she was a Christian and wanted to bless the tables.

'You are not a Christian.' I told her. Then her face contorted, and she started hurling curses at me, yelling at the top of her voice.

"The assistant manager and other employees came out to see what was happening. When she saw the others coming, still yelling, she said she quit and walked out of the restaurant.

"Tony, my assistant manager, looked at me with wide open mouth. I told him to find someone to cover her shift and told everyone else to get back to work. Then I proceeded to reverse her curses and bring the Kingdom atmosphere back into the restaurant.

"I pray in this restaurant several times a week, and we have workers who are believers and pray. But we only do this when the restaurant is closed. Her changing the atmosphere that fast indicates that she was a high-level witch on assignment. She probably had help with others praying on the outside of the building.

"I walked the grounds and discovered various weird-looking items and dead animals hidden in the bushes around the building."

"When was the last time you walked around the building?" Andy asked.

"About a week before this happened," Joshua replied. "Since then, I have assigned people to walk the grounds daily."

"So, you see, Mr. Tom," Joshua continued looking at me with a twinkle in his eye. "Security for an operation such as ours is at another level. We have to be on the lookout for government spies and saboteurs, and we also have to look out for witches and such."

"I see," I said, feeling a bit overwhelmed by what I had just heard.

I know that evil exists, I know about witches, and I have been to several deliverance services. In our small group meetings, I've even helped deliver people from demons and witchcraft, and I have discerned when demons have come out of them and even when they are resisting. But it still amazes me and frankly makes me uneasy to know that this kind of evil exists in the world and that we must be prepared to meet it head-on.

"We do have intercessors in our community who can do that. I'm just not sure the number of people we have will be enough," I continued.

"You will have enough," Mr. Smith said assuredly. "God will raise them up."

I nodded in agreement with what he had just said.

"Hungry?" Joshua asked, changing the subject. "Let me get you menus. Lunch is on me today."

51

We all thanked him as he got up to get the menus. When he brought them back, we ordered lunch.

I noted that the three of us chose foods that were not nutritionally sound. I chose a cheeseburger and onion rings, Andy battered fried fish with French fries, and Mr. Smith decided on nachos with everything on it. We also ordered milkshakes topped with whipped cream and a cherry for dessert.

"I am going to pay for this," Mr. Smith said, sitting back and rubbing his stomach halfway through the meal.

"Um, hmm," Andy agreed.

My burger was not as good as the one I had the day before; it tasted greasier and bland. If I hadn't had the burger at the Co-op, I would not have noticed the distinct difference in quality and flavor. Today's burger is the one almost everyone accepts as a typical burger.

"Yesterday's lunch was much tastier," I said, adding my thoughts to the conversation.

"And healthier," Mr. Smith added.

"You ate at the Co-op?" Andy asked.

"Yep. It was the first real food I have had in a long time." I replied.

"Man, I'd eat there every day if I could."

"What? You don't think every weekend is enough?" Mr. Smith asked his son, teasing him.

"Nope," Andy replied.

We finished our lunch, and all of us were completely stuffed. Joshua walked over and, seeing our lethargic condition, started to laugh.

"I barely eat meals here anymore, even though they are free," Joshua started. "What you feel like now is what I used to experience daily. Bloated, sluggish, full but not satisfied."

"What caused you to stop?" I asked.

"Our church was doing a corporate fast two years ago at the start of the new year. I lost nearly 20 pounds and just felt better overall. When the fast was over, I assumed I would return to how

I ate before the fast. Got to work, ordered some food, took one bite and was like…. nope. Not anymore."

"Do you bring your lunch to work?" I asked.

"Yep. My employees tease me because they can't understand why I would bring food when it's free to eat here."

"We should get going before we fall asleep." Mr. Smith said, starting to get out of the booth. "We have a lot of ground to cover today."

Andy and I got up and followed Mr. Smith and Joshua to the front of the restaurant, where more people were eating. I looked at my watch and saw it was just before 1 p.m.

"Let's walk a couple of blocks before we get into the car." Mr. Smith said after saying goodbye to Joshua.

We walked past a few office complexes, medical offices, and a few more restaurants. We turned the corner which led us to a residential street. A man was mowing his lawn with a push mower. We have seen more and more of them with the high gas prices.

The houses in this neighborhood were more prominent and further apart than where Susie lived, and I could see that some had swimming pools in the backyards. We continued walking until we reached the end of the block. We walked up to a house, and Mr. Smith started walking around to the back of the house. The backyard was enclosed with a large wooden fence. Andy and I followed him.

"Where are we going?" I asked.

"I want to show you something." Mr. Smith said as he pulled a key from under a flower pot and proceeded to open the back gate."

We walked into the backyard, and there was a large pond, about the same size as the swimming pools I observed behind the other homes. Behind the pond was a container garden.

"Whoa!" I said, taking in the backyard. The space was totally transformed.

"Take a look." Mr. Smith instructed, pointing to the pond.

Andy and I both walked over to the pond and looked inside.

"There's fish in there!" I exclaimed.

"Tilapia, actually." Mr. Smith answered.

"So, this is what a fish pond looks like," Andy said.

"How many are in there?" I asked. It looked like the fish were swimming on top of each other.

"Too many." Mr. Smith said. "This is the first time Jack, the house owner, tried this. We're sending some people over tomorrow to go fishing, in a manner of speaking. He introduced too many fish for the size of his pond and called us for help.

"But it's a good beginning. Perhaps the co-op will serve fish next weekend. A nice change from chicken."

"He converted his pool to a pond. He did an amazing job." Andy said as he walked around the pond.

"Amazing is an understatement," I said, surveying his backyard. "You would never know from looking at the front of the house that this oasis was behind the fence!"

"Hidden in plain sight." Mr. Smith added.

"I understand," I said, observing in real time what *hidden in plain sight* means, marveling at the sight of the fish.

My mind was racing, and I was starting to work out various scenarios in my mind on how something like this will work for us back home. I knew of several people who were part of our church community with pools in their backyards.

We walked out of the gate, and Mr. Smith locked it and returned the key to its place under the flower pot.

"Is it safe to leave the key under the flower pot?" I asked.

"He normally doesn't," Mr. Smith said, "but he knew we were stopping by."

"Oh, man! You got me again!" I laugh. "Do the surprises ever stop?"

"As you have already experienced, my dad leans a little to the dramatic side of things," Andy explained as he tilted his body slightly to one side to illustrate.

"Keeps things interesting." Mr. Smith answers back a little defensively.

We walked around the block back to the business district and headed towards the car.

"Tom, do you sense anything?" Mr. Smith asked.

"As a matter of fact, yes. As soon as we came to this busy street. The atmosphere felt different somehow. Heavier. I didn't notice it when we left going into the neighborhood, but I can feel it now."

"It's what Joshua was talking about earlier. The Spiritual pulse he mentioned. Can you discern anything else?"

I stopped walking, standing still for several seconds. Mr. Smith and Andy also stopped walking.

"The atmosphere is definitely heavier. I also hear the word 'comply.'" I paused. "OK, this is going to sound weird but it feels like what it would be like on a Borg cube."

"A what?" Mr. Smith asked.

"Oh, dad." Andy sighed and rolled his eyes. "From *Star Trek*. Remember, we watched one of the movies together."

"The Borg assimilate people into their collective," I continued.

"They have no choice, no free will. They are all of one mind, like a hive mind. They no longer think for themselves as individuals. There is no remorse or regret for their actions when assimilating or killing people.

"One of the famous lines of the Borg is 'resistance is futile.' In the Star Trek Universe, very little can defeat them. I am getting that sense here now, on this street. All of their plans are moving forward, and they believe that no one can stop them and that everyone will comply with the new order of things."

"But they were defeated eventually, weren't they?" Andy asks.

"In the Star Trek universe, only in the Alpha Quadrant where the Federation rule. But they still exist in the Delta Quadrant."

"Yea, I don't know if you can ever completely eliminate evil. But you can sure slow it down and move it out of your way." Andy replied.

"So, how does your analogy apply, Tom?" Mr. Smith asked.

"Well...the Borg didn't consider an individual or even a small group a threat. Individuals were generally ignored, even when they were on the Borg cube. Only when they started messing with their technology did they take notice.

"Not unlike today. Like the house with the fish pond. Hiding in plain sight, as you say. One house with a fish pond or another house with a full garden does not threaten the food corporations' hold on the country's food distribution. So, these 'one-off' situations are basically ignored.

"This 'pulse' that I am sensing is like the Borg in that they are continuing with their plans. They are aware of spiritual opposition but don't consider it a threat, so they ignore it.

"I think it's this arrogance that is going to be their downfall," I said, completing my explanation.

"We are flying under the raider if that's what you mean. "Mr. Smith said. "And it's done on purpose. We don't want to make a big splash, so to speak, and we want all of our plans in place and secured."

"But like in one of the episodes I watched," added Andy, "You know the one I mean….with Hue? The Star Trek Generation story."

I nodded, indicating I knew what he was talking about.

"The Generations crew basically evangelized Hue…a lone Borg found near a crashed Borg vessel," Andy explained to his dad.

"They showed him what it was like to be an individual and gave him a name instead of a designation. They had hoped to disseminate the idea among the other Borg, disrupting their hive mind. They sent him back to the Borg collective."

"And it worked." I continued.

"In another episode, several Borg were freed from the collective. They learned to think for themselves. Because Hue was evangelized with the idea of being an individual with his own ideas, the Borg collective threw him and many others out, believing them to be defective. But the point here is that they were free."

"We have others working in these offices and hospitals. Like

Joshua, they touch many lives." Mr. Smith explained, understanding the connection.

"These people know how to blend in while simultaneously evangelizing and discipling people as the Holy Spirit leads them. We want to win the whole world, but we understand that this is done one person at a time."

Both Andy and I nodded in agreement.

"The Borg were defeated in many episodes. It was their arrogance or narcissism that ultimately caused their defeat. The belief that no one could defeat them. It was their single-mindedness that was their downfall. Maybe that's the same here as well." I said, looking off into the distance.

"Very insightful Tom; thank you for that." Mr. Smith said and then turned to Andy.

"Will you pass this information to the intercessory team since you understand the whole Star Trek thing?"

"Yep, I will," Andy replied, pulling out his phone to text.

We continued walking back towards the restaurant and the car, all deep in thought.

The Country Tour

We drove out of the city for about an hour. We were traveling on a two-lane road. About 30 minutes into the drive, our scenery turned into farmland with rows and rows of corn stalks as far as the eye could see. Occasionally, we could see a different crop, soybeans or barley.

Finally, we started to slow down, and we came to a dirt road with no markings or street signs and made a right turn. We could have easily passed it by, and I wondered how Mr. Smith knew when to take the turn.

"I use the car mile marker to know when to slow down." Mr. Smith said, anticipating the question I didn't have time to ask.

"Hidden in plain sight again?" I said with a twinkle in my eye.

"You got it."

We drove on the dirt road for about a mile. There were corn stalks on both sides of the road. Then the landscape turned into green grass. We could see cows grazing and relaxing under some trees in the distance to the right and left of us. Soon we could see a house up ahead. It was hard to make out, but I thought I saw a man standing in front of the house with a shotgun!

As we got closer, I could definitely see that he had a shotgun in his hand.

"Uh, I think he's holding a shotgun," I said, feeling a bit uneasy.

"Yep. That's Fred for ya." Andy answered.

"Don't worry, he won't shoot us." Mr. Smith said.

We drove up and parked to the left of the house. Fred walked over to us, holding his shotgun against his chest with both hands. The barrow was pointed up at an angle.

"Thought you would be here earlier," Fred said directly to Mr. Smith.

"We were detained. I would have called if you had a cell phone." Mr. Smith said with a smile.

"Yeah, well…. have no use for them out here. Cell reception is not the best."

I checked my phone at his comment and noticed that I had one bar of phone signal fading in and out.

"Meet Tom, Fred." Mr. Smith continued. "Let's show him what you do here."

"Nice to meet ya, young man." Fred took one hand off the riffle and offered it for a handshake.

"You too," I said, shaking his hand tentatively, trying not to stare at the riffle he was holding in his other hand.

He led us to the back of the house. There was an entire garden, but the plants were in the ground like we did on our farm. Further back was a considerable chicken coup and a small barn. I could see several structures on his property spaced out across the landscape. The scenery and the smell of the place reminded me of our family farm.

We walked into the barn. It was surprisingly clean and empty of animals. There were planning boards to the right, and a large oak table was used as a desk to the left. Fred instructed us to sit down, so we pulled chairs from various places close by and sat down.

Fred put the shotgun on the wall back in its place. He had 3 other shotguns hanging, and one appeared to be an antique.

Against the wall, there was a table with 4 monitors showing various parts of the property. One of the monitors was off the main road, where we turned to enter the dirt road that led to Fred's property.

Fred saw me eyeing the monitors.

"There's a wired alarm at each of those points," Fred said, pointing to the monitors.

"When you all turned on my street. The alarm set off."

"But Fred. You knew it was me. Why do you have to meet me with a shotgun every time I come?" Mr. Smith asked.

"Don't know it was you fur sure. Can't never be too careful." Fred said defensively with a hint of a Louisianan southern drawl.

"Well, anyway. Fred was the first farm to join the co-op." Mr. Smith said, leaning back in the chair.

"Yep." Fred picked up where Mr. Smith left off.

"I saw where things were headin'.....with the farms and all, and I didn't want to be a part of it. I wanted to keep my independence."

"What do you mean?" I asked.

"They was tellin' us, the Banks, the distribution centers, and the like that we had to catalog some emissions and such. Well, I looked into it, and they wanted me to track and measure my cow poop with some kind of machine and then report to them that we sell our produce to. And I just could not see a way to do it and remain afloat. But I didn't want to be no sell-out. Just when I was tryin' to figure out what I was goin' to do, I met good ole' Mr. Smith here. To make a long story short, I joined the co-op instead of sellin' out to the big corporations."

"Fred helped us lay the groundwork for other independent farmers to join, and he was instrumental in referring several other farmers," Mr. Smith explained.

"Were those your cows' grazing we saw?" I asked.

"Yep. I got the best and tastiest cows in the area. Best milk and cheese too." Fred replied, beaming.

"The burger you had at the co-op came from one of his cows." Mr. Smith answered. "Although our Chef's seasonings may have also added to the burger tasting so good."

"We buy a full cow from Fred every year." Andy chimed in.

"What do you do differently? That was probably the best burger I had ever eaten." I asked, genuinely curious about Fred's process.

"Well…" Fred started, taking a deep breath. "These cows you see on my land aren't the typical American cow, you see. I use the Guernsey cow for dairy products. And Polzin Pinzgauers for beef. Both A2/A2."

I stared at him with a blank face.

"Most of the cows raised in this country are A1/A1 or sometimes A1/A2. It's a specific gene the cows carry, and my cows carry A2/A2, which is not as common in the United States. Scientific studies show that cows that carry A2/A2 genes are better digested by them that's lactose intolerant. And if you don't pasteurize the milk, it's much more nutritious."

"But isn't it unsafe not to pasteurize?" Andy asks.

"Not if you do it correctly. I sell both pasteurized and unpasteurized milk to the co-op.

"And the beef?" I asked, still wanting to know what made the burger so good.

"My cattle eat grass, turnips, and rutabagas."

"So...you don't feed them corn? Not even as a finish?"

"Nope. No corn here. My cows' milk, cheese, and meat are more nutrient-dense because the cows eat closer to what the Good Lord intended. Although corn is grown, it is a carbohydrate, and too much of it can cause bacteria and disease in the cows. And if the cows are not healthy, neither is what they produce."

"Wow," I said and sighed.

"But I am not sure how we would be able to add cows like yours to our co-op. We would probably have to purchase a farm or start a farm from scratch. Most of the farmers I know already sold out to the corporations."

"We can help with that depending on the plan your community incorporates." Mr. Smith said in a reassuring voice. "We're here because I want you to see first-hand what your options are."

I nodded, thinking about the cows, my burger, and how I would really like to have a burger like that more often.

Andy looked at his watch. "Dad, we'd better get back if you want to make your meeting."

"Oh, yes," Mr. Smith looked at his watch with a frown.

"I was going to have you over to the house for a piece of apple pie," Fred said, disappointed that we weren't staying. "I get my apples from farmer Mike, who owns the apple orchard a few miles away.

"Sorry, Fred. Next time," Mr. Smith said as he got up.

We all walked back to the car. I wasn't too disappointed not to get a piece of pie, still feeling full from lunch. But I wouldn't have minded spending more time on the farm and even touring the apple orchard. It's been a while since I've been on a farm. I didn't realize how much I missed being on one until now.

The City Tour

On the drive back to the city, Mr. Smith took us a different way. We passed another farm that was also part of the co-op. Only the farm didn't have cattle. The farm had lamb and goats. We could see them grazing, the lamb on one side and the goats on the other.

We also drove past property housing 3 beehives. Mr. Smith said they produced some of the best honey he's ever tasted.

We came to a building near the edge of town, where Mr. Smith pulled into the lot and turned to look at me.

"I will see you tomorrow, Tom. Andy is going to take over from here."

"OK," I said. "Thank you. See you tomorrow."

Andy got into the driver's seat, and we pulled out of the parking lot and headed back toward the town.

"Dad's busy all the time with meetings," Andy explained. "The co-op has a lot of moving parts. You're just getting a sense of the food distribution network. But we've developed an entire economy separate from what's out there. To give people a choice, you know what I mean?"

"Yes, I know exactly what you mean."

"We got to get things set up before they tell us we can't."

We drove for about 10 minutes and then pulled into a parking lot. We parked in front of a building that looked like it used to be used for manufacturing. There were no windows on the street level, but there were windows on the top 3rd-floor level.

We got out of the car, walked around the side of the building, and entered using one of the keys on Andy's keyring. There was a large desk with a computer, but no one was sitting there. A sign on the desk said '*Closed*', which listed the open hours as Monday through Friday from 8:30 a.m. to 12:30 p.m. To the side of the desk against the wall were rows of bins and boxes with canned and fresh produce tagged with a yellow sticker.

Beyond the desk was ample open space with rows and rows of…..food! The majority of the food located here was packaged or canned. On the other side of the building, I could see fresh produce.

Fans were hanging from the ceiling, moving in the direction of pulling hot air up. The room was well-ventilated and cool.

"Wow!" I said in amazement. "There's enough food here to feed an army!"

"That's the intent," Andy replied.

"When someone comes to us for help, the food we provide for them comes from this location."

We walked towards the front of the building, and I could see canned vegetables, canned fruit, packaged crackers, cereal, and even cookies. At the front of the building, there looked to be checkout counters like what you see at the grocery store. In front of the counters were shopping carts with the co-op logo.

Andy continued explaining. "When an individual or family comes in, they are allowed to shop in the store. Based on their family size and needs, they are given the row numbers to shop from and quantity of items for each row."

"Do they get a week's worth of food?" I asked.

"Depends on their situation. The case workers make that determination. Some get vouchers that are good for up to 6 months. Usually, not past that time, though. Everyone who comes to us is on a plan. And every plan's priority is to eliminate food insecurity."

"You can get them out of their food insecurity situation in 6 months?"

"Less time than that most of the time. But that does not mean families are completely out of the woods; it's just that they don't have to use this warehouse as their primary source."

"Got it."

We walked to the back of the warehouse. There were rows of freezers like what you see in grocery stores. Here, there were all kinds of packaged meat from the farms. There were also frozen vegetables, some prepared foods, and even frozen desserts, like pies and cakes.

Andy saw me eyeing the pies. "We allow them dessert, but we limit the amount allowed…at least in the beginning. The idea is to ensure the families have their nutritional needs met and not stock up on junk food."

"Where did you get all of this food?"

"The food comes into us almost daily, and the community donates about 10% of what they produce."

"Like a tithe?"

"Exactly. It's how we can keep this place replenished. The door we came in is the same door our community uses to donate their food. You saw the food near the desk, and looking around, it appeared there was not enough room on the shelves. The food has been logged, though. You can tell because of the yellow sticker."

"Is the donation mandatory?"

"Nope. But people want to do it. They want to help. I know one person who gives about half of what she grows. But most people sell their excess food at the co-op, and some will donate what they don't sell."

"Impressive," I said, turning in a circle and taking it all in.

"How many people come through here?"

"Hundreds weekly. There are so many hungry people."

"Do you give food to people even if they don't want to join the co-op?"

Andy sighed at this question. "It's one of the things the leaders will discuss at the meeting my dad's attending. An individual or family is allowed a week's worth of groceries every month if they don't want to participate. Some people feel we should limit the amount to every 3 or 6 months or even a year. Some fear that people are rotating from place to place with no plans of making any life changes. They want to save groceries for people who want to do better for themselves and their families.

"Based on our database, the inventory has been slowly decreasing as the number of people coming for help increases. If they do make a change, this will be the reason."

"The shelves seem pretty full to me," I said, turning in a circle and surveying the many rows of food.

"Yeah…." Andy also turned in a circle looking around, and he had a puzzled look that turned peaceful as he made his full circle. He started walking back towards the side door where we entered, offering no explanation to his puzzled, then peaceful look.

"Hey, do you let co-op members shop here?" I asked as we started walking.

"Yes, but that's also being discussed. Many members will come here instead of going to the co-op for various reasons. The co-op is only open Friday through Sunday, and some people prefer to shop on a different day because of schedule conflicts. The other problem is that co-op members do not have a restriction on what they can buy here. If they have enough community money or credit, they can get whatever they want and as much as they want.

Some leaders are concerned that some food sources will be depleted prematurely unless restrictions are put in place."

"You think they're going to start rationing the food?"

"*I* don't think we should." Emphasis on the 'I'."

Again, he offered no explanation. Andy was lost in thought for a few minutes, and I didn't want to interrupt.

We drove down the street 3 or 4 blocks and then pulled to the side of the road.

"Look over there." Andy pointed to the right. My eyes followed where he was pointing.

There was a large dome-shaped structure sitting by itself on land between houses.

"What is that?" I asked.

"It's a specialty-designed greenhouse, so food can grow in it all year round. They have them in Canada. The co-op purchased one, and we're experimenting on food type and quantity to see how well it will serve the needs of our community."

"Can we take a look inside?"

"Unfortunately, not. The couple in charge is out of town due to a death in their family. We forgot to get the key." Andy frowned. "The co-op should have its own set of keys. I will have to add this to my dad's to-do list."

"OK. I was just curious. I guess I've been in a greenhouse before."

"Yeah, it's not all that exciting in my opinion. But where I am taking you next is *Dope!*"

Andy pulled back into the street and started driving again.

"Oh, by the way. We're going to a house meeting later. *'WFF'* *babie,* worship, food and fellowship." Andy said this, jumping in his seat to an invisible beat, causing the car to rock a little.

I laughed. "Sounds good."

We continued driving for about another 10 minutes. Then to the left, I saw a bank of solar panels and a building about the same size as the warehouse we had just left, except it was a little taller. Andy parked the car right in the front.

Andy opened the locked door with a key on his keyring like he did before. He opened the door, and we stepped inside a tropical botanical garden. The air was hot and humid. There were ceiling fans above, this time turning in the direction to push the warm air down. The ceilings in this building were taller than the last. There were also sizeable industrial-size humidifiers throughout the building. But only some of them were on. Since it was August, there was plenty of natural humidity outside.

There were various tropical plants and trees inside that I did not recognize.

"We are attempting to grow bananas, coconuts, mangos, oranges, lemons, lime, avocados, and pineapple."

"Oh, man!"

"We started this project about 2 years ago. The trees are growing, but they have not yet produced fruit. I think there's also a cinnamon tree somewhere in here."

"This is amazing. Do the solar panels belong to this building?"

"Yep. So far, the solar panels store up enough energy to get through most of the winter."

I started walking down one of the aisles. "This must have cost a fortune."

"I don't exactly know how much," Andy said, following me. "I know that we got some of the seeds from our missionary friends, others we purchased. I think the solar panels help keep the cost down somewhat, and the building we bought really cheap. It was a foreclosure or something; both warehouses were.

"I remember how excited dad was with the purchase. He actually took my mom and spun her around the kitchen dancing."

"Really?!" It was hard to imagine Mr. Smith dancing.

"Yep. I can't wait until these trees have fruit on them! We have a lot of variety in the co-op market, but we don't have everything we're used to just yet. At least not consistently."

"I know. Never thought I would miss a banana."

"Me neither." Andy laughed. "It's been a long time since I had a banana split."

"Yeah, me too!"

"It's really hot in here. We'd better head back to the car." Andy said with beads of sweat forming on his forehead.

"OK."

Multiplication

Andy drove us to an area of the city that was more densely populated. Many of the homes were older, but they were well-kept. As we drove, he pointed out homes that had their own gardens and mentioned they were part of the community. Some homes even had food growing in their front yard. Two houses turned their entire front yard into a food garden. One house had plantings directly in the ground. The other had various size containers.

"How do you know where everyone lives without looking at directions or something?" I asked Andy.

"I'm on the intake committee. I've visited many of these homes. It's part of the process of joining our community. We survey their homes and take soil samples to help them determine their growth strategies."

As we drove, I saw that some of the blocks had plots of land with gardens. *'This city seems really well prepared.'* I thought.

"Your city seems really well prepared," I said out loud what I was thinking.

"Believe it or not, if the entire food distribution network were to shut down tomorrow…. meaning the remaining grocery stores and the like, many people would go hungry, but those in our community would not. But my dad says we represent less than 10% of the city, and he says we can feed about another 3% outside the community consistently. So, there's always a push to help people become self-sufficient."

"Do you know how many people join in a week?"

"I don't know. But we have seen an increase in membership based on what dad has said. But as you know, it takes time to grow a garden and then be able to eat from it.

"We've gone through a lot in the last 5 years, but we also learned a lot. We have people in our community growing food using various techniques. Traditional growing methods, hydroponics, aeroponics, and so on.

"And then there's seed harvesting. We have, I think, 3 houses that do seed harvesting. Two of them, it's all they do. They go around the city to people's houses, gathering seed material from the best plants. It's starting to become a '*thing*.' Growers want their seeds to be picked for seed harvesting, giving them status among the house growers.

I furrowed my brow, thinking. "So, when you got started, were you concerned that everyone would choose to grow the same thing? Do you know what I mean? Did you think the community would have too much of one vegetable?"

"Yep. My dad had anxiety over the community having only lettuce and tomatoes." Andy said.

"But we never had that problem. Since our emphasis was on nutrition, we were teaching people to grow a variety of stuff. Plus, we keep track of who's growing what so we know from week to week how much of a specific item we will have and how long the supplies will last. The information helps our community to determine what to plant more of and possibly what to plant less of.

"The basic amount rarely changes for the family or individual, but the information becomes important for those who sell and trade their additional harvest. Our non-community customers are increasing, and more and more people outside our community are purchasing from the co-op, which skews the numbers a bit."

"Do you think you will continue to keep the co-op open to non-members?"

"I hope so. *I* don't think we will run out of food. I believe the food, even now, is being multiplied. We just don't see it in front of our eyes. But several times, we have seen a massive amount of food leave the warehouse and the co-op. The inventory levels on the database spreadsheets say we're low on this or that. Then we put on an alert, and people are like, what are you talking about? We have plenty of food, and the shelves are full. I think God is really blessing our community. And as the saying goes…we are blessed to be a blessing."

"You think that's happening now? I mean, with the inventory concern?"

Andy sighed. "My dad sees it and believes we will not run out so long as we stick to the Kingdom plan. But there are a couple of leaders who are more by the numbers than by the Spirit. It's been a constant struggle between faith and practice."

"But you can actually *see* that the shelves are full…overflowing even."

"I think my dad will take the leaders on a tour of the facility to show them so they can see for themselves. I hope it will be enough. Anyway, I'd better let Deborah know what's going on." Andy pulled over to the side of the road, pulled out his phone, and started texting.

After Andy finished texting his message to Deborah, he put his hand on the steering wheel, getting ready to pull off, and then hesitated.

"My dad and I weren't sure if we should tell you about another community member who we keep off the books, in a manner of speaking."

I looked at Andy my curiosity peeked.

"Based on our previous conversations, I think it's OK to tell you. It speaks to your Spiritual IQ like what Joshua was talking about."

"Yeah, I've been meaning to ask. What is that?"

"Basically, it's what you are able or willing to comprehend regarding Spiritual matters. If a person sees things more from a natural perspective, that is how we will deal with you. Know what I mean? But you have discernment, and you seem to have some understanding of the supernatural. We didn't want to overwhelm you with that stuff if you weren't ready."

"Yeah, I get it. Still not sure if I'm ready." I laughed nervously. "But I have experienced some things, and I want to understand more. I really do."

"There is a community member who gives away a lot of food from her garden, and I have seen her garden picked bare and no eggs in the hen house because she's given it all away. We were concerned that she put herself back into food insecurity." Andy began explaining.

"The next day, my dad was going to have a *'talk'* with her…." He put his hands up using the quotation gesture.

"When my dad and I got there, several people were in her front yard with various size canvas bags in their hands. Anne was walking out the front door with a canvas bag full of food handing it to one of them.

"We both looked at each other like…what in the world was going on? She saw us and asked us to come inside and out to her backyard." Andy paused, remembering that day.

"Tom, as sure as I am sitting here…her garden was full and ready to be harvested again! My dad and I would not have believed it if we hadn't seen it with our own eyes. Not only that, but she also had about a week's worth of eggs! It was unbelievable!"

My eyes were wide as I looked at him, believing everything he was saying.

"We asked her…well, my dad asked her. 'Cause I was speechless. Anyway, he asked her a one-word question. 'How?' And she said she stood in the garden that night and prayed for multiplication to feed HIS sheep.

"There was more to it than that one prayer, but essentially, Anne does not run out of food. Like never, and it's as if the garden of Eden was re-created in her backyard."

"But you don't tell the community about her garden?" I asked.

"My dad decided to just remove her from the public database. She also told us that when we went in the day before with our unbelief, the garden stopped growing. She had to clear the atmosphere in a manner of speaking. And when she did, the garden replenished itself.

"You noticed she does not let the people inside the house; they remain in the yard. She does this to preserve the atmosphere."

"But don't you think people should know? It would help them increase their faith, and also, there would be more homes with replenished gardens. You know, like when Jesus blessed the fish and loaves of bread and how it fed more than five thousand people."

"We have people in our community at various faith levels…. different spiritual IQs. Some are not even believers. We saw how our unbelief affected her harvest, and we didn't want to risk that again. She was up all night praying after we left."

I pondered what he was saying, not convinced that the community should not be told.

"The other thing that must be considered is how the enemy can come in and attack what God is doing. We wanted to preserve Anne and her ministry. Not everything God is doing is supposed to be out in the open. She's feeding her neighborhood, and many people have been saved and joined the community because of her actions.

"That being said, my dad has recently introduced a few select people to Anne, and she's mentoring them."

"Oh, OK. That makes a lot of sense. Only training those who are ready."

I sat back in my seat, digesting what Andy had just told me. I wondered if anyone in my community was ready for that kind of training. Or even if they would believe me if I told them that it was possible.

Andy put the car in drive, and we pulled off. I looked at my watch, and it was almost 6 p.m.

"Now it's time to have a little fun," Andy said, driving towards the sunset.

The Gathering

We entered a well-maintained, one-story home and were greeted by Jack and Jane. They were an older couple in their late 70s. As we walked in, we could see a crowd already gathering. All looked to be in their 20s and were from various cultural backgrounds. Andy told me that Jack and Jane had been hosting young people at their home for about 3 years. The gatherings are held once a month. Jack and Jane tell their testimony; there's worship, fellowship, and food.

After making introductions, Andy led me to the kitchen, where there were beef patties, sliced chicken, and roast beef with all the fixings to make a sandwich or burger. There were also 3 kinds of cookies to top off our meal. We fixed our plates, got a glass of iced tea, and went to sit in the dining room.

Someone started playing the guitar. We talked to others sitting around the table. Everyone wanted to know who I was and where I lived, and I told them, giving them some insight into what it was like living in my state. We talked about how different it was for us today versus 5 years ago when most of us were teenagers. How the assortment of foods in grocery stores and restaurants has shrunk, the gradual closing of fast-food restaurants, and the stress of not always having enough to eat. Some of us knew we could get a good breakfast and lunch through our schools, but even the school lunch programs started to break down in some parts of the country due to the lack of available food sources.

The gathering was a mixture of young people who had their own family gardens and those who relied on the co-op's outreach programs for food. Some worried about the future and if additional pressure from the local or national government would interfere with the co-op's food independence. Others contemplated leaving the country altogether, believing life would be better elsewhere. The majority seemed hopeful that life would improve because of their faith in God.

After a little while, when we were almost finished eating, Jack and Jane talked to us about what it was like when they were a young couple in their 20s. They told us their perspective of what our country was like in the '70s, '80s, and '90s. They talked to us about their struggles and how they came to know and trust Jesus. They also spoke to us about how they dismissed the signs of the times regarding government control early on. They spoke of how the Church became complacent and dependent on a few leaders to carry the burden of our country, not understanding at that time that it was up to all of us. Jack and Jane wanted us to know so that we would never forget and that it's up to us to grow in the word of God and carry the torch to the next generation.

After they finished speaking, we sang some worship songs with someone on the guitar and another person playing the keyboard. A peaceful heaviness hung in the air while we were worshiping. From experience, I knew it was the presence of the Holy Spirit. Some people raised their hands, and others lay prostrate on the floor. There were times when we went silent with only the keyboard. Other times we sang with no instruments.

Jack prayed us out around 9:30. We said our goodbyes, and Andy drove me back to Susie's.

I repeated the same ritual I did the night before; I wrote about what I saw, the people I met, and the lessons I learned. This time it took me a little longer as I wanted to document some of the conversations I had. I specifically wanted to record the conversation concerning Spiritual IQ and the multiplication of food. I also wanted to capture some of the key points of the conversations I was a part of at Jack and Jane's house.

After writing for more than 2 hours, I put the journal away. I brushed my teeth, put on my pajamas, and got into bed. I turned out the light thinking about supernatural food multiplication.

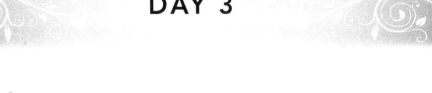

DAY 3

$\mathcal{T}$HE SUN WOKE ME UP again, the same as the day before. I looked at my watch. It was 7:00 a.m. *'Wow, I must have been exhausted,'* I thought. I laid in bed thinking about the last couple of days. I was thankful that I was here. So many thoughts were going through my mind about what I had experienced and seen.

I thought about Joshua's story about the witch who cursed the restaurant. The fish pond in the backyard. The change in atmosphere in the business district. How the food continues to multiply. I decided to share this with my community. Although there will be some who won't believe, I think it will increase the faith of others.

I also thought about the farm. I didn't realize how much I missed working with my dad and my brother. Visiting Fred's farm brought back a lot of memories.

Soon, Susie knocked on my door, announcing breakfast. I quickly got up, showered, dressed, and went to the kitchen. The air smelled of freshly brewed coffee.

"Have a seat," Susie said while flipping pancakes on the stove.

"It smells delicious in here," I said, sitting at the table in the same spot I sat in yesterday.

Susie put a plate of pancakes and eggs in front of me. Butter and maple syrup were already on the table.

"Coffee?" She asked me.

"No, thank you. I love the smell, but I don't drink it."

"Apple juice, then? I just purchased a couple of pints from one of the local apple orchard vendors."

"Yes, that would be great."

Susie poured a glass of apple juice, put it on the table in front of me, and sat down to eat. She said grace for the both of us this time, and we dug into our respective plates.

"I am going to church this morning," Susie began. "You are welcome to come with me, or I can take you to Andrew's church, or you can stay here. I can arrange for Andy to pick you up from here or my church service."

"You don't go to the same church?" I asked.

"No. Andrew goes to Trinity, and I go to Victory. I can't remember the number of churches that are part of the co-op community, but it's a lot. Not to mention the home churches, Mosques, and Synagogues."

"Oh, really!?" I asked, almost choking on my pancakes.

"Yep. We all have the same common goals...to come out of the world's economic system and ensure no one goes hungry. But Andrew can tell you more about that."

"OK." I nodded and continued to eat, making a mental note to ask.

"Anyway," Susie continued. "What would you like to do? You were at Jack and Jane's home church last night, right?"

"Yeah, it was really great. I still feel the peace of the Holy Spirit from the worship." I took a couple more bites.

"I will go with you. I am here to experience as much as I can. Too bad I can't go to both services."

"They meet simultaneously, so that won't be possible."

"Do you ever combine services?"

"Yes, we do. We all gather together a few times a year, usually at Victory. But sometimes at my church, since both churches can accommodate larger gatherings."

We finished eating our breakfast; I put the dishes in the sink, and Susie went to get ready.

When she was ready, we went into the garage and got into her car. She drives a hybrid model, and it looked to be about 5 years old.

"Does your hybrid get good gas mileage?" I asked her.

"It does. I don't drive every day being retired. Once or twice a week at most. So, I don't have to fill the tank as often. I like the fellowship at my church, and so far, God has provided enough to take care of my gas needs so that I don't have to miss church."

We drove for about 15 minutes arriving at Victory about 5 minutes before the 10:00 a.m. service. Susie introduced me to a couple of people before we sat down. As soon as we sat, we were right back up singing worship songs.

Susie's church building holds about 1000 people. There was about a third of that in service today. The message was titled '*Love in Action.*' The pastor referenced the Book of James Ch. 2. He mentioned that their co-op community was doing a lot of good for the city, feeding and providing shelter for people in need. But the church can't become complacent as it had in the past, leaving the work to organizations instead of church people jumping in and doing their part. It's not enough to just donate food or money. We are also responsible for reaching out to our neighbors and fostering relationships in our neighborhoods.

I liked the message. Helping others resonated with me, and I took note of their web page to share it with my community back home.

After service, Susie led me to a small bookstore and coffee shop. We chatted for a few minutes, and then Mr. Andrews came in and joined us. His church is only a few minutes away, and the services typically finish around the same time.

"Hello, Tom and Susie." Mr. Smith said as he sat down with us. Susie got up to get us some drinks.

"Today won't be as long as the last two days." Mr. Smith began.

"I will take you to Deborah's home in a bit. We don't have anything specific planned after you meet with Deborah. We can regroup and summarize your visit over dinner."

"Sounds good."

Susie came back with our drinks. We talked for a few minutes, and several people came by to say hello and introduce themselves. After a few more minutes, we left the church building. Susie headed home, and Mr. Smith and I headed for Deborah's home.

Impartation

Deborah lived in the heart of the city, not too far from the business district where we were the day before. Her house was on a quiet street lined with mature trees.

We parked in the driveway and started walking towards the front door. Before we stepped onto Deborah's front porch, the front door swung open, and a tall woman with salt and pepper hair beamed at us.

"Hello! Hello!" Deborah said.

"Hi, Deborah. How are you? We've talked on the phone a lot, but it's been a while since I've seen you." Mr. Smith said.

"I know!" Deborah sighed and then turned her attention toward me. "Hello, Tom. I've heard quite a bit about you. Welcome."

"Hello. It's nice to meet you."

"I'm not going to stay," Mr. Smith began. "Just wanted to make introductions."

Mr. Smith started to turn back towards the car. "Bye, Tom. Will pick you up later."

"Bye."

Deborah led me into the house. We walked into a spacious living room with contemporary furniture. She led me to the kitchen, where she had food on the table. Contrary to Susie's house, Deborah did not have a lot of plants in her home. But I could see a garden in her backyard through the kitchen window.

"Have a seat, Tom. I prepared lunch for us. I hope you like tomato soup and grilled cheese sandwiches."

"Yes, I do." I sat down in the chair, Deborah indicated.

"The tomatoes came from my garden out back. Growing up, I used to love to eat tomato soup and grilled cheese sandwiches. So, I taught myself how to make soup. I hope you like it."

"I'm sure I will. It looks delicious."

Deborah brought over two bowls of soup for us and sat down to my left. Deborah said grace, and we began to eat.

The soup really was delicious, and so was the grilled cheese sandwich. The bread was rustic with a lot of crust, and the slices were cut thicker, which was nice because there was a lot of cheese between the bread slices. We both had water to drink.

We were silent while eating, enjoying the blended taste of the soup and cheese sandwiches. Other than the distant sound of birds chirping outside, we could only hear the sound of crunching bread and clinking spoons.

I am usually a little nervous when I first meet someone, especially eating in someone's presence. But I was very comfortable eating in silence with Deborah; it was as if we'd been eating together like this for years. It wasn't that I was uncomfortable eating with Mr. Smith, Andy, or even Susie. It was just more relaxing with Deborah somehow.

Deborah finished eating before I did since I opted for a second grilled cheese sandwich. She sat back in her chair, rubbing her stomach in a satisfied manner, smiling at me.

"How has your visit been so far?" Deborah asked.

"Really good," I said in-between bites. "Very informative and eye-opening."

"Eye-opening? How so?"

"Well, I guess I mean seeing the possibilities of what can be done. The creativity and also the intricacy of how everything fits together."

Deborah nodded in thought, still looking at me. Then she smiled and began clearing away the dishes. By this time, I had finished my sandwich.

"Let's sit in the living room. I was thinking about sitting outside on the deck, but it's hot today."

I followed her to the living room and sat in an oversized armchair. It was very comfortable. I pulled out my notebook and pen from my backpack and waited for Deborah to begin. Now, I was a little anxious. I wanted to hear what she had to say, but at the same time, I somehow knew my responsibility was about to increase greatly because of the Spiritual knowledge she was about to impart.

"I thought I would start from the beginning." Deborah began.

"I was called to intercession many years ago. But we won't go back that far." Deborah smiled and winked at me.

"When Andrew.....Mr. Smith, had the tent meeting a few years ago, I was there. I was also there when he had the first meetings at the church. Everyone was concerned about the practical side of things. The classes, the gardens, etc. And I was right there with them. There were no specific plans for prayer or anything. Nor were there any plans at that time to put something in place.

"This went on for about a year or so. There were hiccups along the way, but we saw them as part of the learning curve and the normal process when you start something new. But things began to gradually get more challenging. People disagreed more. Some families were leaving the community for various reasons.... petty arguments, and offenses.

"Also, some of the family gardens were not growing as expected, and we couldn't figure out why since they were all using the same process. We would send people to their homes to test the soil and check their water usage, but we could not directly point a finger as to why some gardens were more successful than others."

Deborah took a sip of the water she had brought with her into the living room. She was sitting on the corner of the sofa closest to me.

"It's still a little shocking to me that I didn't see things clearly right away. I mean, I was trained as an intercessor, and I didn't even suggest that we pray about what was happening.

"I had gotten so frustrated with how everything was going that I was thinking of dropping out."

Deborah took another sip of her water, deep in thought.

"What made you change your mind?" I asked her, very curious about what happened next.

"Well," She blinked, coming back to the present. "It was a random Sunday in the Spring, I think. We were worshiping at the beginning of the service like we usually do. Then a heavy anointing fell on us, and we worshiped the entire service. There was no message, just spontaneous worship. It was pretty awesome.

"After that service…later that day, in fact, I had a strong knowing in my Spirit that I was supposed to stay in the community and that I was to initiate prayer strategies for all of the issues we were having.

"I talked with Andrew about this, and he agreed. By the way, Andrew was also at that service. Many people in the community at that time were in that service. The service gave us a new sense of purpose and understanding of our purpose.

"It was like our eyes were opened, and we could see how the enemy crept in and was trying to tear us apart."

Deborah then looked at me and said, "He rarely comes at you head-on; He comes more like a snake. Slithering his way in just out of immediate eyesight to catch you off guard. This is what happened to us."

Deborah paused, and I wrote in my notebook.

Her words brought back a flood of memories and situations regarding my family. How many times were we caught off guard?

"Our intercessory team was just me at first. But it didn't take long to build a team," Deborah continued. I re-directed my attention back to what she was saying.

"During this time, we discussed the community's intake process. In the beginning, basically, anyone could join….and it's still that way to a point. But now we do screen those who want to join. We learned the hard way that first year, but it allowed us to learn from our mistakes.

"One of the processes we implemented was visiting the homes as part of the intake process. This would allow us to help each individual and family devise a plan best suited for their needs."

"I decided to go with Andrew and another intake team member to visit a new member. When we entered their home, I noticed it was clean and stylish. But there was a funny feeling in the air, and Andrew noticed it too. So, I gently started asking questions. How long had they lived there, how long have they been married…that sort of thing. Then I turned and saw a foreign idol sitting on their mantle. Funny that I didn't see it when we came in. I asked them about it, and they explained that a friend had given it to them as a wedding gift.

"I told them what I was feeling in the Spirit and suggested that the foreign statue might be the cause of it. I asked if they had any other items. They mentioned that they had a couple of other pieces in their bedroom and went to get them.

"The darkness coming from all of these objects…. especially since they were all in the same room together, was really heavy. I knew, and Andrew confirmed. We suggested that they get rid of these pieces, and they agreed to do so.

"I then prayed for the couple and the atmosphere. And that was that."

Deborah sighed and continued.

"From that point, we realized that we should include a Seer… someone who sees and discerns in the Spirit….to go on every house visit. In putting this in process, we decided to return to the families already part of the community. We started with the homes that were having trouble with their harvest."

She turned and looked at me again. I didn't realize that I was staring at her, fascinated by her account.

"This is where it gets interesting." Deborah shifted in her seat and continued.

"There were three homes that were having trouble growing food. I didn't put two and two together before…. but all three homes were within a mile radius of each other. We visited all three but didn't get anything specific. When I got home, I continued to pray, and I heard in the Spirit the word *'battle.'* Still not sure what that meant, so I kept praying.

"Well, I ended up at the library for something unrelated a couple of days later. I walked by a row of books on the history of our city. One of the books caught my eye. Can't remember the title, but it was about the history of the indigenous people who lived in this area before there was a city. I opened the book and read that there were several battles where our city is now. One tribe against another, and later battles between indigenous people and the settlers. The book was pretty specific as to where the battles took place. Do you know why?"

"No," I said, intently listening.

"Because when digging the ground for building homes…. they found the burial grounds. Mass graves. And do you know where those graves were?"

"In the same area as the three homes?"

"Yes! The same one-mile radius! Back then, they buried people where the battles were, and it was not like they would take them to a funeral home or something. So, God showed me what happened and why their plants were not growing. Basically, the ground was cursed because of the massive amount of violence."

Deborah reached for her Bible that was lying on the coffee table. In it were several handwritten sheets of paper.

"The verse that came up in my Spirit was Romans 8:22-23. But I love this quote by Harry Alan Hahne, who puts it this way:

> *'Both believers and nature groan together as they long to be set free from the consequences of sin. This solidarity is an inescapable consequence of the dominion God gave humans over nature. Thus, when human beings sin, the natural world for which humans have responsibility is negatively impacted.'*

"Hahne wrote a paper titled '*The Whole Creation Has Been Groaning.*' Basically, he wrote we not only have a responsibility to get people saved, but we also have to save the earth. When humanity sins, it affects nature; it affects the earth.

"I was getting Spiritual insight as to what happened. But the question remained...how do we fix the problem?"

"I'd never considered that nature could be damaged by our actions. What *did* you do?" I asked, mystified.

"Well...I prayed for strategy. But before I tell you what we did, I want to stress that every situation you encounter will be different and calls for a strategy directly from Heaven. Nothing that I tell you today should be made into a rule or format. The worst thing you can do is create a religion around these strategies." She was looking at me intently.

I nodded. "I understand."

Deborah nodded once and continued.

"The strategy God gave me was to get two more people so that there were three of us and walk the mile radius praying in the Spirit once a day for 3 days. We were not supposed to pray in English, only in our heavenly languages. So, I chose 2 other people I knew flowed with speaking in the Spirit, and we did as instructed."

Deborah opened her Bible again.

"In the same chapter in Romans, verse 26 and 27 says this:

> 'At the same time the Spirit also helps us in our weakness, because we don't know how to pray for what we need. But the Spirit intercedes along with our groans that cannot be expressed in words. The one who searches our hearts knows what the Spirit has in mind. The Spirit intercedes for God's people the way God wants him to.'

"I like to confirm what I hear from the Holy Spirit with scripture. It keeps me grounded.

"Anyway, we walked the mile radius, but nothing really happened. I didn't get revelation, and neither did the people who walked with me.

"About 3 days after that, I ran into one of the women who lived in one of the affected houses. We spotted one another shopping at the Co-op. She came up to me excited. She said that the lettuce she had been trying to grow started to come up. She also attempted to grow various herbs, but the seeds didn't seem to sprout. They were now sprouting. Everything she planted that wasn't growing before was now starting to grow!"

"Amazing!" I said, sitting back in my chair.

"Yes, it was amazing. I contacted the other families, and it was the same for them as well. Their gardens were growing, and today, all of their gardens produce excellent results.

"Andrew was really excited to hear the results. He spoke with the other leaders, and they made my role as Head Intercessor official."

"So, you head up the Intercessors and also the Watchmen?" I asked.

"Yes. Well, technically, everyone is a Watchman in our community, and we ask everyone to keep an eye out for anything out of the ordinary. However, some are more seasoned and spiritually mature, so we assign them to certain areas. I believe you've met some of them?"

"Yes, I met Joshua, Joe, and Margie."

Deborah nodded. "They keep me informed about what's happening in their territory."

"By territory, you mean where they're assigned? Like Margie with the restaurant? Joe with the co-op arena?"

"Exactly. I meet with the Watchmen once a week. But they call or text me if I need to be aware of something. So, I have several meetings a week. The Watchmen, the Inner Circle, the Prayer Leaders, and then a prayer meeting that is open to anyone."

"The Inner Circle?"

"There's five of us," Deborah said as she nodded to my question.

"The Inner Circle meets weekly, and we pray over sensitive topics. It could be personal prayer requests from the leadership or strategies we don't want to be made known to the public.

"Then I also have a prayer meeting with other Prayer Leaders in our community. We talk about strategy and what is happening within their respective meetings. This is also where each leader will tell us what prophetic words, dreams, visions, words of knowledge, and discernments have been spoken in their meetings. It's really cool to put the prophetic pieces together, and it helps us get a clearer picture of what God is saying to us on a specific matter.

"I also give them prayer points based on what's discussed in the leadership meetings, the Inner Circle, and how the Holy Spirit leads me.

"Lastly, we have a weekly prayer meeting on Wednesdays at the church open to anyone who wants to attend."

"Does your community pray around the clock?"

"Not a lot. Today, we have prayer meetings 7 days a week, either in person, online, or over the phone. Over the years, we've occasionally had 24, 48, or 72-hour prayers.

"But we didn't start out this way. We can pray 7 days a week because we've grown and have enough people to do so."

I was taking notes as she was speaking.

"Do you chronicle your prayers?"

"Yes, as a matter of fact, we do. We have a vault on the community intranet where our public prayer sessions are available to listen to. We also publish testimonies, which you can look up using keywords."

I nodded. Deborah continued talking.

"We consistently pray for the community families' protection and abundant harvest in the individual gardens. We also pray for multiplication. We are seeing this happen, and we continue to pray so that it becomes commonplace."

"Andy told me about the multiplication of food. That's pretty awesome."

"Yes, it is. Our goal is that our community operates like the Kingdom of Heaven. Thy will be done on Earth as it is in Heaven. It's been a privilege to figure out what that looks like. We've seen many miracles. Not just in food multiplication, either. We've had people's bank accounts multiply. We've also experienced many, many healings.

"Despite what's happening in our country and the world around us, we're pretty content. Happy even. We don't lack for our needs. Some have had to adjust - downsizing to smaller homes and selling off items they no longer need. Some share their homes or rent out a bedroom or two. It's been an adjustment for some but compared to what others are going through out there.... it's been easy for us."

"Do you think that was because your community started forming years ago?"

"Yes, I do. We always knew that the goal was bringing Kingdom to earth, and what you see is our humble attempt to put Kingdom operation in action."

"Seems to me you're doing a good job of it. But the process is not set in stone, it seems?" It was kind of a question and a statement at the same time.

"Exactly. There's a flow to it, and we try not to sit on one methodology.

"When we train our families and farmers about praying and blessing their harvest, we show them multiple ways. We teach them - or at least try to - how to hear the voice of the Holy Spirit and get a strategy that way. But we also stress that the soil was created for its specific purpose, and it's not a pet that you have to train. The land knows what it is supposed to do.

"Sometimes, it needs help in returning to its created purpose. Like the example, I shared about those who lived in the war zone.

"In many cases, it's necessary to ask God to forgive the past sins and actions that took place on the land and then rededicate the land to the Kingdom of God. We've also had some people play worship music over their gardens daily. Others read scripture over their gardens daily. Some make and read decrees. Others talk to their plants. These practices are undoubtedly OK to do. Some of our families swear by their processes. Since people live in different parts of the city, some in older homes, some newer, the process for one will not be the same for another.

"We've explained in our trainings not to take a form or process and turn it into a religion. Kingdom does not work that way."

Deborah sighed, thinking about her last statement.

"I am telling you all of this so that whatever you decide to do in your community, it does not get you bound up. It's important to allow for the creativity of the Holy Spirit and to understand HIS timing of how and when you do things.

"Do you have any more questions for me?" Deborah asked, looking at me with a smile.

"Yes…you mentioned that you have prayer seven days a week but didn't start that way. How did you start? How many days a week? Was there a certain prayer strategy you used in the beginning?"

"I won't tell you the specific prayer strategy we used because I believe the Holy Spirit will give you a different approach based on your community's situation.

"I don't think the specific day you chose to gather for prayer matters. But I do believe consistency matters. I also think leaving room in your prayer meetings to hear from the Holy Spirit and document what He's saying is important. Don't just go into your meetings with a list of prayer requests. Learn to listen and hear what He wants to say to you. This is good to do even in your personal prayer time."

"We do have several people who would likely be the ones who would lead prayer. But how does a person become a Watchman? I mean, how do we make that decision?" I asked, thinking about all of our main praying people, and none seemed to be like the Watchmen I've observed here.

"Probably, the people you are thinking about are not your watchmen," Deborah said thoughtfully.

"It's likely that your watchmen have not yet fully grown into their positions."

Deborah stopped talking for a minute, holding her nearly empty glass of water. Then she continued.

"I want to be careful with how I say what I am about to say. I will tell you, but I think the conversation will have to happen between the Kingdom Coordinators."

"OK," I said, my eyes wide again, waiting in anticipation.

"Many Christian organizations, large and small, run their groups like a corporation, and they use organizational charts and the like to determine who does what. So, these people on the organizational chart perform their 'jobs'...."

Deborah did the quotation sign with her hands.

"But they don't leave much room to partner with the Holy Spirit; To partner with God. I am sensing that your community has some of this ideology as part of its makeup. Resistant to change."

"There is Form, and then there's Substance. The Substance is God, Jesus, and the Holy Spirit. The Form is the religious services, the structures, rules, processes, and procedures. You can have created the 'Form' to contain the Substance, but over time, the Substance becomes restrained.

"I can tell you that the Holy Spirit does not like to be restrained. So, the Substance will leave. The Form eventually becomes empty of Substance, so the only things left are the services or processes. Devoid of the Power of God.

"Yes, I think I understand what you are saying. My community is definitely resistant to change. We have seen our situation gradually worsening and not improving, and our KC has recognized that something needs to change. But we have many people who are very slow to change.

"Before I was chosen to come here, there was a lot of discussion about who should come. Some of our leaders felt like they should have been chosen, and I did feel a little uncomfortable around one or two of them."

"Yeah, people can be unfortunate obstacles to getting in the way of what God wants to do. So, part of your initial prayer strategies may be to deal with the perceived barriers.

"I will make sure our prayer team prays for your community."

"That will be greatly appreciated," I said with a sigh, thinking about what will happen when I bring back my report. Based on what I have observed here, we will have to make drastic changes in how we do things, and I think there will be several people who won't like that.

Deborah continued, "Our goal is to be the head, not the tail. We want the world to come to us for advice and strategies. We want to be an example to the world and its' systems. In all of what we're doing, we keep the bigger picture in mind….' Thy Kingdom Come, Thy will be done on Earth as it is in Heaven.'

"Start first with you, then your family, then your community. Pretty soon, a whole city, then a state, and then a country can and will be transformed. God has no limits; The only limits are what we put on ourselves."

"Yes! And Amen!" I said, suddenly feeling excited about the possibilities.

Deborah's phone chimed. She looked at it and then at me.

"Andrew is on his way to pick you up. He'll be here in about 15 minutes."

"OK," I said, disappointed that our meeting was ending.

Soon, Mr. Smith was ringing the doorbell. Deborah and I exchanged numbers, hugged, and said our goodbyes.

Dinner

"So, how was your visit with Deborah?" Mr. Smith asked as we drove away.

"Really good," I said, thinking back on the afternoon. "Informative and enlightening. Deborah has a very calming Spirit, and she reminds me a lot of my mother when times were good."

"That she does." Mr. Smith agreed.

"So, where are we going now, Mr. Smith?" I was curious about dinner plans.

"Oh, you can call me Andrew, Tom. We've spent a lot of time together this weekend getting to know one another, and I think we can now be on a first-name basis."

"OK…. Andrew. Where are we going? Are you taking me back to Susie's?"

"Nope. I thought for your last night with us, you could share a meal with my family. I'm taking you to my home."

"Awesome!"

We drove for about 10 minutes and arrived at Andrew's home. The home was on the corner of a quiet street with mature trees. We drove into his driveway from the side street, where an older model car was parked on one side. The driveway was lower than the front entrance of his home, equal to the backyard level. The backyard was fenced, so I couldn't see into it. Andrew pressed a button inside the car, and the double-car garage door opened. We drove inside. There was another Tesla parked inside the garage.

We got out and went inside. The door opened into a large room with patio doors to the backyard. Andrew led me out the patio doors. There was a patio with a table, chairs, and a grill. Beyond the patio was a large yard turned into a garden. There were some containers with plants, but other areas of the yard had rows of produce growing directly from the ground. I could recognize corn and tomatoes immediately.

"This is *our* garden." Andrew said, emphasizing the word 'our.' "This is what started it all. But when we began, we didn't have as much produce as we do now, and back then, we only used half the yard."

The backyard was big. Probably about a quarter of an acre, I estimated in my head. In the center of the yard was a paved circle edged with flowers, outdoor lounge chairs, and a fire pit. From the paved circle, there were several paths leading to the various rows of produce.

"Really, really nice," I said, looking around in awe. "What do you do for irrigation?"

"We installed underground sprinklers. When we decided to turn the entire space into a garden, we drew up some plans and strategically placed the sprinklers. We also have the sprinklers set on a timer, and we only turn it off when we know we're going to get plenty of rain.

"We also installed a cistern on the side of the house to catch rainwater." Andrew pointed to the cistern partially covered by bushes.

"We have not yet had a need to use the rainwater, but we went ahead and installed it just in case. That way, if the city restricts watering, we would have rainwater as a backup."

"Wouldn't the only reason to restrict watering be because of a drought?"

"We had three people on different prayer teams dream about water restrictions. We believe God was warning us that the enemy was trying to slow our progress in growing food. So, Deborah instituted prayer strategies around this. So far, so good. No restrictions.

"However, Judith, my wife, and I decided to purchase the cistern anyway. Not from a lack of faith; We just wanted to see how much we can move off the grid living in the city."

"Oh, yeah. Do you have solar panels?"

"We do. We also have a generator." He pointed to a caged generator at the back of the house."

We went back inside the house. The room was large, with a sectional sofa, built-in bookshelves, and a large television. There was also a kitchen area, a bedroom, and a full bathroom on this level.

Andrew led me up the stairs, where we entered a hallway into the living area. We were greeted at the door by a middle-aged brown Labrador.

"Hi Fanny," Andrew said to the dog, rubbing her head in greeting.

We entered the kitchen, where I met Andrew's wife, Judith, and his daughter Jenna. Andy entered the room, and we all sat at the kitchen table, and Fanny laid down in the threshold of the kitchen watching us.

"Dinner is almost ready," Jenna said.

"Andy and Jenna prepared dinner this evening. They are both outstanding cooks." Andrew said.

"Still a fight to get them to clean up after themselves," Judith said with a wink.

Andy and Jenna told me some funny stories referencing their journey from fast food to gardening and cooking.

After a while, Jenna got up and checked the oven.

"Food's ready!" Jenna said in a loud voice as if we were in another room.

Andy and Jenna prepared our plates. Judith poured iced mint tea into glasses and set them on the table.

"Do you like white meat or dark meat?" Jenna asked me.

"Dark meat, please," I responded.

She sat our plates in front of us. Andrew brought silverware to the table.

"Everything we eat is from the co-op or our garden," Andy explained.

"We have herb-baked chicken, peas and carrots, and scalloped potatoes. The chicken came from Fred's farm, and we grew the peas, carrots, and potatoes. The rolls came from the co-op. Mom made strawberry and rhubarb pie. The flour and sugar also came from the co-op. I prepared the peas and carrots. Jenna prepared the chicken and scalloped potatoes."

"My contribution was purchasing the rolls, flour, and sugar from the co-op," Andrew said with a wink.

Andrew said grace, and we began to eat.

"How do you come by the sugar and flour?" I asked.

"Two of our wheat farms have their own mills, and they sell the flour in various forms at the co-op.

"Regarding the sugar, we have a relationship with sugar farms in Texas and Louisiana. Sugar was one of the commodities we started accumulating right away in case there was a breakdown in transportation. It is one of our more expensive items at the co-op because of transportation costs. We also have some co-op members that grow beets and produce their own sugar. Some sell beet sugar at the co-op. It is less expensive than cane sugar since it is locally grown. That being said, we're experimenting with growing sugar cane in the hot house. I believe you saw the tropical warehouse on your tour with Andy."

"Oh, yeah. That was really cool...and really hot." I started laughing at what I had just said.

Nodding and smiling at my comment, Andrew continued.

"We are moving toward being completely self-sufficient for all of our basic needs."

I continued eating, contemplating what Andrew said. The idea of a community, or even a town being completely self-sufficient and not relying on the normal distribution channels for basic necessities. It was exciting to witness a community so close to this reality.

But I wonder if it is too late for our community to become one hundred percent self-sufficient since we waited so long to get started. I live in a more draconian state. Would they try to stop us from being self-sufficient somehow? Andrew's community is in the open with almost everything they do. Would we be able to do the same and get away with it?

"I've been thinking about a plan for your community and what it would look like," Andrew said as if he read my mind.

"I think your community will have to be a little more covert, considering your state's political position. We can help you diversify your home gardens for their nutritional components. And then perhaps neighborhood house meetings and church meetings where you trade your goods with each other. We can then use back door routes for other goods like your meats and other commodities.

"But honestly, Tom. Depending on what happens with the next election, everyone in your community may have to seriously consider relocating to a different state. Perhaps, relocating here. I want you to know that you and everyone in your community would be welcome, and we will make room for you if it becomes necessary."

"I appreciate that."

I remember our move from the farm. It was not easy. The idea of having to move again….and possibly out of state was not something I wanted to think about. And if I'm having a hard time with it, I know most of our community would also have a hard time. But I knew what Mr. Smith…. Andrew was trying to say. Pretty soon, it might not be safe to live where we are now.

We finished our meal, deciding to wait on dessert. Andrew suggested we sit on the deck. It was early evening, with a light breeze in the air. Their deck was positioned off the kitchen overlooking the backyard. The back of their house faced East. Although there was still light, the sun was no longer shining on the deck.

We all sat outside, including Fanny, who lay next to Andrew's chair, where he occasionally reached down to stroke her head and back.

Andrew began.

"Do you have any questions for us?"

"Oh, I am sure I will have a lot of questions later. I am still taking it all in. But I think I can make an encouraging report to our KC. You have all accomplished so much here. I'm just sorry our leaders couldn't see what was coming earlier."

"Yeah, in the beginning, it was hard," Jenna said. "I remember truly believing our dad had lost his mind. Andy and I used to hang out with our friends and get pizza or fast food almost every weekend. Then dad told us we could no longer do that. Man…. I went into my room and cried."

"Jenna and I used to have private meetings in one of our bedrooms." Andy continued. "Dad told us to journal our experiences, so we decided to do this on social media. At first, we were sort of complaining about our situation. But then people started asking us questions like they were truly interested in our journey."

"Oh, I thought the social media thing happened after you stopped complaining," Andrew said, looking puzzled.

"Nope. We were going to tell the world how ridiculous you were. But we found out that you were a genius instead." Jenna said, beaming at Andrew.

Andy continued, "Yeah, we became popular really quick. That was surprising. But it showed that more people were ready to make changes than we thought."

"How did you feel about making your own lunches and preparing dinner?" I asked them both.

"At the time, it added insult to injury," Andy said.

"But it wasn't so bad once we got into it," Jenna said. "The biggest thing was that we could not hang out with our friends during the experiment to ensure we were only eating our planned meals and not sneaking pizza. It felt like we were being punished when we did nothing wrong."

"Bottom line, you both were spoiled. But that was your dad's and my fault. We wanted to use the experiment to un-spoil you. And I think we succeeded." Judith said with a wink.

"It wasn't as bad as I thought it would be, and I felt better with the food we were eating. But I was also glad when it was over so I could hang out with my friends again." Jenna responded.

Jenna raised her eyebrows and spoke again. "Our journey did help me gain a better understanding of the Bible. God created the earth to take care of us, and he created man to take care of the earth. I didn't really see the connection until we started this journey. Many of the examples and references made are around food and farming. Our experience gave me a deeper appreciation for many of the passages; how they speak to our relationship with the earth and God."

Andrew and Judith nodded in agreement and smiled at their daughter, pleased with her insight.

After a few more minutes of talking, Judith returned to the house and brought us a plate with a warm piece of pie and a scoop of vanilla ice cream. We ate for a few minutes in silence.

"That was really good," I said, breaking the silence.

"Thank you," Judith replied.

Andrew finished the last bite of his pie and started talking again.

"This started because the Lord said we needed a safety net for food. But I realized through revelation and the prophets within the community that what we have started is so much more than that.

"We were creating a physical manifestation of the government of God on the earth. We are taking back territory for the Kingdom. What I mean by territory is not only just land but finances, spiritual well-being, and health. We recognize and seize from the enemy dominion and everything else he has stolen and transfer it back to the Kingdom of God.

"When your community partners with us, more territory is taken back for the Kingdom. We are pushing back the darkness but strategically. We take the offensive position, catching the enemy off guard so that it's too late by the time he realizes what's happened.

"After that, our job is not to give him any opportunity to take back what we have taken from him. All creation belongs to God. Basically, we are just kicking out the squatter.

"How will that work for my community? Taking the offensive position since we are so late in getting started?" I asked.

Andrew said, "Deborah and her team are already praying for

your community for specific information and strategies. I believe you will play a major part in how your community develops."

"Your help and prayers are really appreciated," I said.

I was thinking that if things changed for the better, perhaps my brother would want to come home and help us.

"Well…." Andrew stood up, stretching. "It's time we get you back to Susie's so you can get some rest before you travel back…. Oh, I almost forgot!"

Andrew rushed back into the house. The rest of us looked at each other inquisitively. Andrew returned about a minute later carrying a satchel with the community logo on it.

He handed me the satchel.

"I almost forgot. These are our most successful air loom seeds for various fruits and vegetables, and we chose the ones that will flourish in your growing zone. These seeds are blessed and have been prayed over, so I don't doubt you will have an abundant harvest to feed your growing community."

I took the satchel, nodding my thanks.

"Good night, and thank you," I said as I hugged the family.

Andrew and I headed back downstairs to the car. We got in and drove to Susie's. We sat in the car for a minute.

"Thank you again, Andrew, for everything. I learned a lot in the past couple of days. I was unsure of what to expect when I arrived. Everyone has been so open, friendly, and loving, even. I really felt at home the entire visit. I only hope and pray that our community can become what yours has succeeded in doing by developing a Kingdom community."

"You're welcome, Tom. But I am sure this is not the last time we will see or speak to one other. There's still a lot of work for all of us ahead. Your community and ours are partners now. And you are part of this community regardless of what happens in yours. Please remember that."

I nodded, unable to speak because of the lump forming in my throat.

"Susie said she would take you to the train station in the morning. Goodnight Tom. Have a safe journey home."

I nodded again, got out of the car, and headed up to Susie's door, which was already opened in anticipation of my arrival.

I performed the same ritual I had done the two nights before. I sat down at the desk and reviewed the notes I had taken while meeting with Deborah. I added a few more thoughts from the dinner, put on my pajamas, brushed my teeth, and went to bed.

During the night, I had a dream about my community. In the dream, Larry, our community KC was pulling a cart by himself like he was an ox. The cart was very heavy, and he was struggling. He strained, but the cart only moved a couple of inches forward. I looked to see what was in the cart, and it was weighted down with several huge bundles. The bundles had labels on them. I struggled to see what the labels said. I saw two or three that were labeled 'complaints.' A couple of them were marked 'doubt', and several others were labeled 'fear.' I also saw some labeled 'judgmental,' 'jealousy,' and 'stingy.'

I looked to see where Larry was trying to take the cart. Ahead, I could see a mountain top. The image zoomed into view like you would see in a camera. I could see a garden on top of the mountain, which resembled what could have been the Garden of Eden. The garden was peaceful, and there were all kinds of plants with fruits and vegetables. There was a meadow with several animals running about free and happy.

My gaze turned back to Larry. He was sweating from the strain of pulling the cart. But his eyes were on the mountaintop, and he knew that was where he wanted to get to. Then he stopped pulling, turned to look at me in the dream, and then I woke up.

I pondered the dream for a while and fell back to sleep.

THE RETURN

*T*HE NEXT MORNING, I WOKE, got up, and showered while Susie prepared a hearty breakfast. Pancakes, eggs, and turkey sausage. She also packed a lunch for the trip that included 4 sandwiches, two slices of pie, cookies, sweet potato chips, and 6 bottles of water. The packed lunch was heavy because of the water, but I didn't mind. I was grateful to have more than enough.

"There should be enough to share with another person. The divine encounter you will have on the way back." Susie said.

"You think I will meet someone on the train ride back?" I asked.

"Never know," Susie said with a wink.

We got in her car, and she drove to the train station. There were already many people there with their luggage, gathering to make their trips to various parts of the country.

I thanked Susie for her hospitality, hugged her, and walked into the throng of people...one of the hundreds going to various destinations.

I knew that even though I was heading back to my community, the destination I was heading to was very different from the one I had come from. The destination was supposed to be the mountaintop I saw in my dream. Visiting Andrew and his community has given me the key to helping Larry and our community get to that mountaintop.

I walked onto the train with a renewed sense of purpose and determination. *'We will get there,'* I thought to myself. But it was more than a thought; It was a knowing. We were going to get to the mountaintop.

ENDNOTES

Prologue

1. Felder, S Renee. *The Bridge, Moving from Increasing Chaos to Future Peace*. Self-Published, 2019. The book is a prophetic word about the banking system in the United States. The how and why the banks will collapse, and its effects on our daily lives.

2. Lonnie Parton, Victory Fellowship Church, Council Bluffs, IA. https://www.victoryfellowship.church/

3. Nichols, Jim. Last modified June 12, 2022. https://livestream.com/accounts/12411424/events/10478938/videos/231629117. Victory Fellowship Church, Council Bluffs, IA. The connection between the tallit and the Tabernacle.

4. Reed, Chris. "Chris Reed Unveils Prophetic Warning About the Coming 'Perfect Storm' in America." www.charismanews.com. Last modified April 5, 2022. https://www.charismanews.com/culture/88825-chris-reed-unveils-prophetic-warning-about-the-coming-perfect-storm-for-america.

5. Stone, Perry. "The Coming Apocalyptic Food Shortages." Perry Stone Ministries. Last modified September 16, 2022. https://www.youtube.com/watch?v=xEc7dMxLMf8. Biblical and natural signs that point to food shortages around the world.

6. Giles, Joshua. *Prophetic Forecast* (pp.96-97). Minneapolis: Chosen, 2022. Prophecy of a famine, and crop failures due to extreme drought conditions that will also negatively affect cattle.

7. Johnson, Nita. *Prepare for the Winds of Change II* (pp. 159-160). Clovis: Eagle's Nest Publishing, 1998. Blocks long bread lines and severe lack of foodstuffs.

8. Destiny Image. *Provision in Times of Famine|Chuck Pierce*. Last modified 7/8/2022. https://www.youtube.com/watch?v=fosNYLAPo2Y Chuck Pierce shares how the next 7 years will be intense similar to the story of Elijah and the Shunammite woman.

9. *Genesis Ch. 41:1-7, Bible: New King James Version*. Thomas Nelson, 1982, www.biblegateway.com/passage/?search=Genesis+41&version= NKJV. Pharaoh's dream.

10. *Genesis Ch. 41:33-39, Bible: New King James Version*. Thomas Nelson, 1982, www.biblegateway.com/passage/?search=Genesis+41&version=NKJV.

Day 1 – From the Beginning

11. The Story of Joseph. *Genesis Ch. 41, Bible: New King James Version*. Thomas Nelson, 1982, www.biblegateway.com/passage/?search= Genesis+41&version=NKJV.

12. *Ephesians Ch. 1:18-23, Bible: Amplified*. Thomas Nelson, 1982.

13. *"21 ESSENTIAL MINERALS AND 16 TRACE MINERALS YOUR BODY ABSOLUTELY NEEDS." NUTRITIONAL INFO & STUDIES, 29 Apr. 2019, juicing-for-health.com/essential-minerals*.

Day 2 – The Interview

14. Elvy, Craig. *"Star Trek: Hugh Borg's Backstory Explained (& Why He's Important To Picard)." 4 Aug. 2019, screenrant.com/star-trek-hugh-borg-tng-backstory-picard-important/*.

Day 2 – The Country Tour

15. Metropulos MS, RDN, Megan, and Natalie Butler R.D., L.D. "The benefits and risks of A2 milk." 25 July 2017, www.medicalnewstoday.com/articles/318577.

16. *Polzin Pinzgauer Beef, www.polzinpinzgauerbeef.com/index.html.*

Day 3 – Impartation

17. *Hane, Harry Alan. "The Whole Creation Has Been Groaning." docslib.org/doc/12970634/the-whole-creation-has-been-groaning-by-harry-alan-hahne.*

18. *Federalprism.com,* federalprism.com/what-does-it-mean-the-whole-creation-groans/#:~:text=Both%20believers%20and%20nature%20groan%20together%20as%20they,for%20which%20humans%20have%20responsibility%20is%20negativ.

19. *Romans Ch. 8:22-23, Bible: New King James Version.* Thomas Nelson, 1982, www.biblegateway.com/passage/?search=Genesis+41&version=NKJV.

20. *Romans Ch. 8:26-27, Bible: New King James Version.* Thomas Nelson, 1982, www.biblegateway.com/passage/?search=Genesis+41&version=NKJV.

ABOUT THE AUTHOR

Sonja began receiving prophecies from the Lord shortly after dedicating her life to Jesus in the mid-1990s. As her relationship with the Lord grew, so did her prophetic gift. Around 2006, the prophecies Sonja received from the Lord started to include messages about the Church and the United States. Per the Lord's instructions, Sonja began documenting many of her prophecies on an online blog. Sonja believes Omaha, Nebraska, and the surrounding region will be pivotal to what God is doing for this nation in the coming days.

Sonja wrote and published her first book, *The Bridge, Moving from Increasing Chaos to Future Peace,* in 2019. The first book is a prophetic word about the banking system in the United States.

Currently, Sonja resides in Omaha, Nebraska, where she owns and operates a Tax Firm. Sonja can be contacted via email at josephcolony@protonmail.com.